BACKDOOR VIRGINS

VIRGINS

ALEXANDER MCNICOL

Backdoor Virgins
Past Venus Press
London 2005

Past Venus Press
is an imprint of
THE *Erotic* Print Society
EPS, 1st Floor, 17 Harwood Road,
LONDON SW6 4QP

Tel: +44 (0) 207 736 5800
Email: eros@eroticprints.org
Web: www.eroticprints.org

© 2005 MacHo Ltd, London UK

ISBN : 1-904989-17-9

Printed and bound in Spain by BookPrint S.L., Barcelona

BACKDOOR VIRGINS

ALEXANDER MCNICOL

EPS

Chapter 1

When Ellen was a child, her mother and father had always just called it 'the Cabin'.

Set in magnificent woodlands and overlooking the majestic river that once carried timber down from the mountain logging stations, the Cabin was an idyllic holiday retreat for a family. As well as various utility rooms, it boasted a large living room, a kitchen and three double bedrooms with bathrooms *en suite*. Not the average log cabin in the woods, perhaps, but even then Daddy Roeberd had been a rich man and not one to stint on luxuries. That was twenty years ago. Now Roeberd Inc was a huge conglomerate owning great tracts of forestry, as well as sawmills and paper mills, transport and construction companies. When Daddy Roeberd died last year he'd left his beloved only child a very rich orphan indeed.

Ellen cast a sidelong glance at the big man driving the rental car she had booked at Wenatchee airport. He was good-looking, she thought, in a rugged sort of way. Jim Murray worked for Roeberds as area manager. He had made his way up through the company ranks and was now directly answerable to Meredith Fielding. Who just happened to be Ellen's husband.

Still relatively junior in the company's hierarchy, Meredith Fielding had nevertheless been given a place on the board – as the boss's new son-in-law. Since the old man's death, six months ago, he had been overseeing the restructuring of the Roeberds forestry holdings near the town of Wenatchee and commuting to Seattle every weekend to be with his wife. However Ellen had felt that it was time to surprise her darling husband and, instead of waiting for him to arrive in Seattle, she booked a flight to Wenatchee. Instead of going to Meredith's apartment in town, she had asked Jim Murray to drive her directly the Cabin, the car groaning with groceries and goodies she had brought with her from Seattle especially for the weekend.

The drive had taken forty minutes from the airport. Ellen was feeling excited at the prospect of preparing her man a delicious, romantic dinner, then calling him at work and getting him to drive out to the Cabin from the company office in Wenatchee.

"Were you expecting company this weekend, Ma'am?"

They had been chatting about not much in particular and Ellen was brought up short by this apparently inconsequential question. But she followed Jim's gaze and immediately saw the two cars parked outside in the Cabin's little drive.

"No... I don't believe I was... how strange!"

Jim slowed the car to a halt and got out, shutting his door quietly. He leaned back and spoke to her through the car window.

"Stay here, Mrs. Fielding. I'd better just check this out." Jim Murray's voice was deep and somehow very reassuring.

She watched him walk towards the house. On impulse, she got out and followed, joining the big man as he crouched by one of the bedroom windows, which was half-open. Now she could hear what he could hear. Not the noise of thieves or vandals despoiling the house, but the sound of a man and a woman making ecstatic love.

"Fuck me, big boy, fuck the shit out of me..."

"I'm gonna come, Nancy, damn it if I'm not gonna come for a second time..."

"Hell, me too honey, but you come in my cunt. I want you to fuck me up my shitter, too. You man enough for that?"

"Give me time, hon, just give me time..."

"Ohhh now, honey, now!" the woman said urgently and the man groaned with pleasure as he, too, reached his climax.

She didn't recognize the woman's voice. But the man's was familiar. It was her husband's.

Crouching at the window, Ellen and Jim could make out the couple on the outsized bed. They could see that the girl had a mane of flame-red hair and that Meredith had just collapsed on top of her, his bottom still thrusting spastically, as if pumping the last of his spunk deep into the redhead's twitching cunt.

Then he rolled off her and they kissed affectionately, facing each other on their sides. Ellen froze, as if poleaxed. All she could think of, it seemed, was that the girl's bush was as red as the hair on her head. A very natural redhead, she thought. Cute ass, too. But her tits are too big for that skinny frame. Why – they're even bigger than mine, in fact those hooters are fucking enormous!

But wait a minute! Just wait a fucking minute! thought Ellen. The guy, the man, the dude she's kissing so affectionately, like they've been screwing each other for months – that's my fucking husband, no pun intended...

She became vaguely aware of something, or someone, plucking at her sleeve. She was about to brush them off when she realised that it was Jim. The man was trying to pull her away.

"No!" she mouthed silently, wagging her finger and furiously indicating that he should go back and wait in the car.

Ellen crouched at the window for a long time, maybe twenty minutes. She half hoped that the couple would turn around and see her. But they never did. Instead the one he had called Nancy sat up and made Meredith stand in front of her. Ellen could see that she was making his penis hard again by taking it between her vast breasts to give it a gently enveloping massage. She put a finger into her red-bushed cunt and drew it out, dripping. She slowly inserted the cum-slick finger into Meredith's ass. Meredith groaned. He was hard again.

Quickly, she got on all fours, her own behind stuck high in the air and her head cradled in her arms. Still managing to look back at him, she waggled her buns suggestively, even pulling her pert asscheeks apart so that he could not miss the *café-au-lait* pucker of her anal opening.

"Come on sugar, now fuck me in the ass. I want to feel that big cock of yours fuck my little shitter…"

Ellen was appalled at the crudeness of their language. She and Meredith never spoke in this obscene way when they made love. Yet here he was with this… this freckly, copper-cunted slut, apparently loving her sewer talk.

Meredith placed the tip of his long penis

at the centre of her brown star and pushed. Ellen watched as Nancy once more reached behind her and guided the stiff cock in, inch by inch until his pubic bone slapped against her upturned, vulnerable asscheeks and prevented any further progress. Nancy appeared to love it, ecstatically thrusting back and pulling away. Ellen's husband had a look of bliss on his face as well, a look she knew only too well, but one she hadn't seen for some time now. Indeed, almost as long as he had been out here in Wenatchee. The tears rolled down her cheeks. The bastard! The fucking asshole! She trusted him so much that she never even thought for a second that he would have done this to her. Which is why it came as a total shock.

Jim was back. He led her, sobbing, back to the car, his arm thrown protectively around her shoulders.

All the while Ellen was trying to make up her mind whether to bust in there and give her husband his marching orders. Or wait until he came back to his apartment in Wenatchee and give them to him there. Or pretend it never happened.

She did none of these things. She asked Jim to drive her back to his place. When he started to demur, she looked at him with pleading eyes. He gave in to her and eventually veered off the road down a forestry track to a modest timber frame house.

* * *

She wiped her eyes, folded the dainty white handkerchief and placed it back in her purse.

"It's not just the cheating," she said. "Don't you realize how this makes me feel? For Christ's sake, am I such a goddamn dog that he'd have to go looking for another woman?"

Jim Murray looked at Ellen Fielding critically. He saw a beautiful young brunette in her late twenties with a perfectly proportioned figure, legs that went on forever, a voluptuous, but firm ass and tits that were big enough to make him salivate even in their dressed state. He shook his head.

"No," he said, laughing, "you are definitely not a member of the canine species, Mrs. Fielding."

"Oh, please call me Ellen," she said, laughing with him. "And do you have any booze? Jesus, I need a drink!"

* * *

There was an old-fashioned leather couch in front of a big window in Jim's den where they were sitting. While he fixed her drink, Ellen leaned back on it, noting with surprise that the bookshelves were full of interesting novels, some very recent. A rack of long-playing classical and jazz records sat next to the record player on the table nearby. Although a man of few words, Jim was no backwoods boy. He obviously read good books and listened to sophisticated music. Ellen was intrigued. They chatted while she nursed the bourbon on the rocks he had given her. Jim Murray poured a little more booze into it. He freshened his own drink, too, and looked at her intently while she talked about Meredith and their marriage.

"Are you staring at me?" she asked, self-consciously, giggling slightly. It was much too early in the day to be drinking, and the whisky had gone straight to her head. On the other hand, it felt pretty damn good to be giddy and carefree, after what she'd just been through.

He grinned.

"Yeah, I'm staring," he said, with a rare grin. "A cat may look at a queen, and what's more, you're definitely worth staring at, Ellen Fielding." The big man put down his glass. "I can't imagine where in the hell your husband's mind is. A man that would cheat on you probably doesn't deserve to have a cock."

She laughed and put down her own glass, tilting her head as she stared back at him.

"I really had no idea he was fooling around with Nancy McGuinness," Jim said, "If it's any consolation, she seems to have screwed half the men in Wenatchee. She's not short of admirers and she keeps trying to move up the social register – she's an ambitious little tyke. Her dad, Sean, is now too old to rein her in. He's a big local landowner: it's inevitable he would do business with your husband sooner or later, so that's probably how they met."

There was one of those long pauses, where nothing was actually said, but the look between them spoke volumes.

With a natural confidence that Ellen loved, Jim Murray put his hand on her knee, just below the hem of her short skirt. She felt the warmth of him flow into her flesh.

"Are you trying to build up my self-confidence?" she asked slowly. Her eyes moved up and down his body. She saw the shape of a hard cock at his crotch, protruding a good eight inches down his left leg. Maybe more.

He guided her hand onto his cock.

"I think you just have," she whispered.

He nodded.

"I hope you're in good shape," Ellen said, squeezing hard at his cock-bulge. "I may be more than you can handle."

She stood up, breathing hard. The taste of the whisky was in her throat, but that wasn't why she felt so heated up.

She had led a sheltered life, with a strict and protective father. She'd only had a couple of men before Meredith, and she had stayed a virgin till she was twenty-one.

But she'd come to love sex and the lack of it had been driving her crazy. Masturbation couldn't kill the fires that smouldered inside her, but she'd never have dreamed of cheating on her husband – until now.

Jim watched, idly caressing the erected length of his cock, as Ellen undressed. She made a production of it, taking off her skirt first and showing her long, slim legs, the stockings and garters, the skimpy lace of her delicate panties. Turning, she undid her blouse, then turned toward him, exposing her tits in their flimsy silk bra.

She came toward him, a little wobbly from the drinks, and she let his hands discover her body. Their mouths connected and they kissed bruisingly, passionately, Jim's tongue spearing aggressively into her receptive mouth. She held his big head between her slender hands for a moment, searching his face.

He really wasn't bad looking, she decided, thrusting her tits into his hands. Good, clean features, a resolute jaw and well-defined lips that looked as if they had been carved out of marble. He had the sort of powerful build and determined demeanour that some men would see as threatening, dangerous even. But to Ellen he seemed to be a protector, a comforter, someone who would look after her.

Even with her heels on, she was three or four inches shorter than he, and Jim appeared to be in pretty good shape; he wore his big frame easily. She supposed the heavy, well-developed muscles of his upper torso came from his time as lumberjack. She eased the jacket off his shoulders while he was undoing her bra. It came loose, and her tits spilled out. "Jesus!" he gasped.

She knew that, overall, she was prettier than the redhead bitch Meredith was fucking. Of course, Nancy had an ass that looked pretty good on her skinny frame, those unbelievably huge tits and tight little ass, while Ellen's tits were smaller and her ass was definitely more on the generous side. And the session in the woods proved that the bitch had no qualms about sharing that lively little ass with Ellen's husband.

Ellen had watched, amazed, as Nancy had guided Meredith's hard cock into her ass and he had fucked her wildly up her rectum. It was something he'd often suggested to Ellen, but she'd never been quite brave enough to try it. Besides, it seemed like it might be messy and unhygienic.

Jim Murray quickly took her mind off her gloomy musings. As soon as her tits were bare, he started to suck them. He sucked hungrily while she fed her resilient tits in and out of his mouth.

Ellen swayed while Jim mouthed her tits. She stroked his head, urging him to get nastier. She guided his hand down into her crotch and showed him what she meant.

His fingers slipped inside her skimpy panties and she purred as he caressed the elegant brunette's thick bush until he found the slit of her pussy. It was wet and slippery, her clit erect and yearning. His fingers were a little rough, but Ellen didn't mind a bit. She squeezed her thighs together on his hand and rocked back and forth, eagerly masturbating herself on his thrilling fingers.

"Yes," she said. "Oh yes, yesssss!"

He eased a finger into her cunt and she gasped aloud. She'd almost forgotten what the touch of a strange hand felt like on her cunt. He added another finger to the stirring, and he worked them in and out of Ellen, making her cunt positively drip with musky juices.

Jim pulled down her panties, and she wiggled her feet out of them. He leaned back, looking up at her with eyes full of lust and admiration. His second appraisal of this beautiful girl was no less admiring. Ellen nude was far more delectable than Ellen dressed. He loved the way that the heavy orbs of her large breasts hung off her ribcage, appearing to defy gravity. His eyes devoured the big, dark areolas and nipples that capped them, the gentle curve of her belly, interrupted by the tiny hollow of her navel, ending with the luscious delta of dark brown pubic hair at its base. He looked at her long legs, the flair of her hips, the springy bounce of her resilient ass cheeks, then back up to the thick, glossy mane of fashionably cut chestnut hair that framed her beautiful face: huge grey eyes, a little serious, perhaps, a cute nose and luscious lips, set above a determined little chin, that always just begged to be kissed.

"You're fucking gorgeous," he said, his voice a little choked with emotion. "A man would need to be crazy..."

He stood up, and she let her hands move up and down his body. She opened his shirt, leaning in to bury her lips in the hairs on his chest. She'd never really cared for a hairy chest before, but now she found it thrilling, nuzzling him, tasting the flavour of his flesh, the sweat that was oozing from his pores.

She licked his nipples the way he'd licked . hers, and she felt them harden against her tongue. Her body kept brushing his, and she shivered at the sensation of his hard cock touching her. Easing down onto her knees, she opened his pants and yanked them down, trousers and shorts both coming down together.

His cock sprang out and slapped her lustfully in the face. It was a really big prick, uncut. She had never seen an uncircumcised penis up close before, and certainly not one that was erect. Maybe nine or ten inches, she thought. Much bigger than Meredith's, and there was nothing much wrong with his; she nearly giggled. Ellen took it in both hands and began to stroke up and down the length of his cock, purring with anticipation.

She played with the foreskin, her big grey eyes now shining and wide with sheer delight and wonder, like a child with a new toy. Utterly fascinated, she slipped the loose flesh back and forth over the shining pinkish-mauve knob until his cock had grown so long and stiff and hard that the foreskin would no longer cover its bloated cock-head.

Impulsively she kissed the tip of his cock, pressing her lips against the drooling piss-slit. She left smudges of lipstick on him, but now his knob was so dark and engorged with blood these were hard to see. Ellen parted her lips slightly and rubbed him against the soft membrane of the inside of her cheek, humming as she began to mouth his cock more seriously.

He sank down onto the couch, his legs spread. She slid forward, still on her knees, her mouth glued to his prick. Her mouth was salivating like crazy now. Until Meredith, she'd never enjoyed taking a man's cock in her mouth, but he'd gotten her addicted to the feel and taste of his prick in her mouth, and now she thirsted for it.

Her mouth ovalled, then slid down over the end of Jim Murray's prick. She made a gasping sound as she took him inside her mouth, and her saliva flowed down the shaft to wet his balls while she sucked on his glans.

"Mmmmmm!" she purred over and over, moving his cock in and out of her mouth in short, hungry gulps.

He gave a blissful sigh, letting her take control.

She pulled it from her mouth, licked him up and down. She moved down, lapping his balls as well. A hair stuck to her tongue and she scraped it loose with her teeth, spitting it out and returning to his balls. Pushing them aside, she licked into the crack of his ass. Her hand was playing with his prick, and she felt it get even harder.

She slurped up the length of Jim's cock, up to the big, helmet-shaped knob, as if she were sampling the most delicious ice cream.

Ellen sucked and licked him knowingly, spending a lot of time on the sensitive 'drawstring' just below his bloated cock-head, flicking it repeatedly with the tip of her stiffened tongue. She stroked his prick up and down while she licked it, and a little bubble of clear precum oozed from the little hole at the tip. She caught it on her tongue and savoured the sweet taste.

"Your precum is delicious!" she told him coquettishly. "Now – are you going to fill my mouth up with the real McCoy, Mr Murray?"

"You bet your sweet ass I am," he growled back at her, putting a hand atop her head and urging her down upon his cock.

Ellen smiled and sucked it back inside. She couldn't deep throat a cock, but she could do a damn good job, and she was determined to prove it. This man knew that her husband had ditched her for a redheaded slut. She was determined to show him that Meredith was a complete idiot.

She gulped at his cock, pulling him deeper, massaging his hard meat with the wet warm muscles of her cheeks and jaws. Her tongue worked vigorously, and she moaned as she sucked. He was big, and hard, and his meat filled her mouth. She had never tasted anything so delicious in her life, and she had never needed to eat a cock as much as she needed it right now.

Ellen thirsted for his cum, and she sucked hard, urging it from his balls. Her hands were all over his body, and he was feeling her too, pinching at the stiff red points of her nipples, making her whine and squirm as she ate him.

"Oh, baby, you're gonna get it! Gonna get you a big mouthful!" he moaned as he tweaked her nipples and pushed his prick into her mouth.

She sucked faster, drawing her mouth in around him, and she took his prick as deep as she could manage.

"Now, girl, here it comes!" he gasped, and grabbed her head with both his big, rough hands, holding her steady while he pumped his prick into her. She opened wide and sucked it in, and the spurting gush of his orgasm began. His jizz squirted down her throat. She guzzled greedily, hot for the slimy juice.

"Aaaaahhhh!" Ellen groaned, eating his load. She jerked on the shaft of his cock, milking the thick soupy spunk out of him and into her mouth. She adored the taste: it was so thick and warm in her throat, and she gulped and moaned and sucked until he quit shooting.

Meredith's cock usually got soft in her mouth after it had emptied its load, but Jim Murray's prick remained hard and firm across her tongue. Her big grey eyes lit up with arousal, and she sucked him hard, making sure he stayed stiff.

"Now you have to fuck me," she said, raising her face from his hard cock. "Now you have to fuck my ass off!"

Chapter 2

He pulled her upward, his hands filling with her hot, sweat-damp tits. Ellen climbed on top of Jim Murray, grinding her excited body down upon his. Her mouth covered his. She sucked his tongue the way she'd sucked his cock, and beneath her body, she could feel his prick, as big, as hard, and as eager for her pussy as it had been for her mouth.

"You just passed one of the tests," she whispered. "I won't fuck a man who doesn't want to kiss me after I've sucked him off!"

He kissed her again, spearing his tongue into her mouth, and once more tasting the flavour of his own spunk mixed with her sweet saliva.

"This should guarantee me a piece of ass, then," he said. His hands went down to cup the cheeks of her ass. She squirmed lewdly atop him, spreading her legs to enfold him. The swollen length of his prick rubbed through her dark-furred crotch, stimulating the already-dripping lips of Ellen's cunt.

"I wanna fuck you so bad I can taste it," Jim Murray said. "So why the hell don't you let me taste it for real, girl?"

He pulled firmly on her asscheeks, and

Ellen shrieked in glee, sliding forward. She rubbed her wet cunt across his chest, bringing it toward his waiting face. He opened her with his thumbs, thrust his mouth upward, and began to lick the splayed coral-pink trench of Ellen's aroused pussy.

She rode high and eager above him, squirming and squealing as his licking made her clit throb and twitch in response. He sucked at the hot bud, nibbling it oh-so-gently with his teeth, sending white-hot jolts of sexual frenzy through the woman's body. The tips of his thumbs moved onto the super-sensitive slickness of her cunt-slit, and one of them entered her wet pussy. He thrust as he nibbled her clit, and she screamed in growing abandon.

"Oh, fuck me, you horny bastard! Eat me, and then fuck meeeeeee!"

He fucked his thumb in and out of her, still chewing and sucking and licking and kissing her clit. She came twice, drenching his face with her juices, and he kept on eating, lapping at her steaming pussy as if he were in a contest at some rural county fair.

"Your husband ought to be strung up by the balls!" he gasped, his tongue sliding up and down her cunt-slit. "You got a cunt that tastes like peaches and cream, girl! Mmmm, and now I'm gonna fill it with some hot cream of my own!"

He took his thumb out of her and sucked the juices off it.

Looking up at her, he said, "I guess you still feel like fucking, don't you, Ellen? I mean I can call you Ellen, can't I?"

"You can call me a nasty fucking cunt, if you want to," she said, "just as long as you get that cock inside me!"

"Naaw, couldn't do that. Your cunt's a beautiful thing and so are you," Murray laughed. "But get your ass off my face and I'll give you what you seem to need."

Ellen couldn't remember ever being so excited about a sexual encounter.

She slid back down Jim Murray's body.

"I'm fucking you, stud," she said, lifting herself above his stiff cock. She rubbed the tip through her dripping pussy. "It feels so nice and horny like that! Let me see how it feels inside!"

She eased the cock-knob into her hungry cunt and slid downward, swallowing him with her pussy even more urgently than she'd gobbled with her mouth.

"Ohhh!" she gasped when his cockhead jolted her cervix.

His body stiffened beneath her as she took his entire cock into her pussy. She strained downward, writhing above his groin. He put a hand on her tits, another on her ass, and he began to fuck hard, straight up into her cunt.

He thrust hard, piercingly, filling Ellen's pussy again and again with the swollen meat of his cock. It was hard to believe she'd only just sucked him to a blistering, gushing orgasm. He was stiff and eager, and she was easily as wet and eager to receive him. The knob of his cock fucked deep into her belly, stirring her cunt frantically.

Ellen swamped his cock with her steamy cunt, riding down to gulp him home time after time. She rocked as she fucked him, and she clutched at her tits, moaning and shuddering and coming down the shaft of his prick.

"Aaaaahhhh!" Jim gasped beneath her.

She could feel the mounting excitement throbbing through his cock-shaft. It matched the fiery arousal that bubbled inside her cunt. She met him stroke for stroke, grinding her cunt down onto his prick, eating it to the balls repeatedly.

She came twice more while she rode him.

She leaned forward, moving her tits across his chest. He caught them, squeezing the plush mounds, bringing them to his lips for more bites and sucks and kisses. She moaned, her arms around his neck, pulling him closer to her hard, hot nipples.

"Suck them!" she moaned. "Oh, hurt my tits… it feels so good!"

His cock swelled inside her cunt. It feels so fucking big, she thought, my pussy might rip open. But he didn't miss a stroke, and she didn't miss a stroke, either.

The fucking wasn't as fast, as jackhammer-like, as it had been at the start. They were down to the slow grinding phase now, but slow didn't mean dull. The head of Jim Murray's prick powered continually into the lusting maw of Ellen Fielding's pussy, and she gasped and moaned and whimpered, feeling yet another climax building inside her.

She ground her hungry pussy against him, accentuating the pressure on her ready-to-bust clit.

"You son of a bitch!" she shrieked, rotating her pussy around his prick. "Oh, you're making me come!"

"Me too, you lovely piece of cunt, you beautiful little slut!" Murray cried, getting a wicked thrill out of addressing this elegant, powerful woman in such demeaning terms. A sudden thrust almost sent Ellen into orbit. He pushed his cock to the very bottom of her cunt, held it there for what seemed an eternity, and then she felt him explode.

His sperm blasted into her. He fucked her until his cock went dry. She collapsed on him, her body soaked with sweat, his hands sliding up and down her body until they settled on her quivering asscheeks.

His chest hair was matted with sweat beneath her tingling nipples. She sighed, making her tits move through his moist fur, increasing the amount of stimulation that her rigid nipples already felt.

Jim's cum was oozing out of her pussy, and his cock, going soft, had just begun to slide out of her sticky-wet hole. She sighed again, squeezing with her cunt muscles, but it was too late to trap him. His prick eased out, and after it bubbled the driblets of spunk he had squirted up Ellen.

"You saw them both at the cabin," she said, her voice quivering with an almost hysterical lust. "I told you my husband fucked that little red-haired cunt three times, three different ways. I want a man who doesn't know when to quit. I want a man who can fuck my mouth and my pussy and then roll me over and fuck me again. How about it? Are you that kind of man? Can you get that cock hard and fuck me one more time?"

She didn't give him time to answer. She grabbed his cum-slimed cock and began to masturbate it. She was forceful. Pressing her mouth against his, she slipped her tongue between his lips and ran it around the interior while she continued to jerk on his cock.

"Right here, right now!" she whispered into his mouth, still working on his prick. "I want it again! I've gone without for too damn long!"

He panted, and she could see concentration

in his eyes.

"You're something, lady," he said as his prick began to swell inside Ellen's fist. He put his hands on her shoulders and sat her up, rising with her. "Okay, you horny young bitch, you've got this thing hard again, so I'll just have to let you have it one more time."

He was on his knees beside her now, his prick sticking up at a sharp angle. It felt a little thinner than before, as if she'd somehow compressed it inside her tight pussy, but it was as hard as steel, and she slid her fingertips up and down the length of it, her eyes bright with excitement. She'd never done it three times in a row before, not even with Meredith, but this certainly seemed like a day for firsts.

Ellen bent down to lick it. He still tasted of cum, but there was also the flavour of cunt on his prick. Her cunt. Her juices. She lapped up and down his shaft, nibbling and sucking at the hot spongy glans. Her lips seemed glued to Jim's prick. She sucked it a little deeper into her mouth, momentarily unwilling to stop sucking on it.

But she raised her head, licking her lips, and her mouth glistened lasciviously as she looked up at Jim Murray. He pulled her upright and burned her mouth in a kiss, his hand automatically dropping to her pussy. She sighed into his mouth, arching her cunt into his clutching hand. His finger entered her, poking about tentatively, testing the wetness, the desire within.

"Unh-huh," she said wriggling out of his embrace. "You saw what they did, baby. I want the same thing that freckle-faced slut gave my husband. I never let Meredith fuck me up the ass – not one time – and now I'm going to let you have my asshole cherry, just for proving to me what a shit my husband is. The one thing he never got from me is yours!"

"Are you sure?" he asked, but she could see the new fire in his eyes. "Are you sure you want my big hard cock up that cute ass of yours?"

She lay facedown on the couch, looking up at him over her shoulder. One of her long legs dangled down to the floor, and her crotch was totally exposed to his eyes. She saw him staring at her, and she liked the way he stared. She also liked the way his prick continued to stick up.

"Hurry, before I change my mind," she said. "I'm not sure I'll like it, but I have to do it. I must."

He slid off the couch, onto his knees on the floor. He cupped her nearest tit while he leant down to lick and kiss the curve of her ass. The wet smacking of his lips sent vibrations through her ass and she began to writhe and squirm on the sofa. Reaching down, she fingered her clit as he tongued her ass, and the vibrations continued. She liked that a lot.

He spread her asscheeks and licked playfully at the brown star of her anus. She had a finger up her cunt by now, sliding it in and out of her wet, sensitized fuck-hole. She turned slightly so she could move her finger more freely. He followed with his head and kept on tonguing her asshole.

His tongue moved back and forth from her anal pucker to the lower edge of her pussy-crack. As her finger moved in and out, he licked it too. She slipped the finger out and his tongue poked inside her cunt, stirring her juices just a little more. Then he was back at her asshole.

Jim Murray's licking my bottom hole now, Ellen thought, and it's an incredible feeling. I've never had a man's tongue anywhere near there before, because even though she was always immaculately clean 'back there' it always seemed kinda dirty, fooling around with the place she shat from, but not now. Oh no...

Jim's rough, broad woodsman's hands had her asscheeks spread wide and as he dipped his tongue in and out her anal sphincter gradually dilated more and more. She rocked on the sofa, and kept pushing her ass at his face. The feeling was indescribably good.

"Yes!" she gasped. "Oh baby, please do it... tongue my... my... shit-hole!" said Ellen, feeling wonderfully wicked just by saying that filthy word.

Her eyes got big as he replaced his tongue with his finger. Relaxed as she was, this was an entirely different sensation for Ellen. Something solid pushing gently in where normally things only ever came out. She moaned when the finger, well lubricated by his saliva, continued its inexorable progress, sliding through the still tightly clenched sphincter until suddenly it entered her, bursting into the roomier space of her rectum. Jim started to rotate his finger inside the lovely woman's shit-hole, turning it this way and that. Her anal ring only tightened in response, but he kept up his gentle probing, eliciting more moans of surprise and pleasure as he advanced further and further into the warm, buttery depths of her rectal cavity.

"Loosen up, bitch," he said.

"I'm trying!" Ellen panted, frigging her hot clit in desperation.

His fingertip pushed even deeper, and she made a small nervous sound, but the panic faded quickly, once she got used to the feel of him inside her ass.

She was tight, and involuntarily she fought this unnatural invasion of her bowels. She strained, as if she was trying to shit, anxious to take him despite her sudden misgivings. And then her resistance broke down, and his finger plunged all the way up her asshole. He ground the flat of his palm against her ass-ring, rotating and wiggling his finger inside her, and she whined and whimpered.

He reamed her mercilessly. But with each rotation, her asshole got a little less tight, just as she became a little more excited.

He pulled out of her ass, wiping his finger on an asscheek.

"Okay, baby," he said, "you wanted the real thing, and that's what I'm gonna give you. Stroke my cock once more for luck, and then I'll fuck your tight sweet ass!"

She was still frigging and fingering herself, but she took his cock in her other hand and squeezed, feeling the excited surges that raced through his stiffened meat. He felt a lot bigger than he had a couple of minutes ago.

He mounted the sofa behind her, coming down upon Ellen. She spread a little wider, reaching back with both hands to pull her asscheeks wide open for him.

"Fuck me!" she moaned, "Fuck me up the ass, just like my idiot husband fucked his little red-headed whore!"

He brought the knob of his cock to bear against her asshole. She closed her eyes, feeling its blunt snout nosing her there.

"Oh, come on!" she panted. "Do it to me, stud!"

Her hole was dilated from the finger

reaming he'd given her, and he was able to get the head of his cock inside her with no trouble.

"Oooooh, it's gonna hurt so much!" she whimpered.

"Just relax, push down like you were taking a dump and it really won't hurt a bit," Jim Murray said and, seconds later, drove his cock deep into her bowels, taking Ellen's anal virginity with one powerful thrust.

She screamed at the unexpected force of his sudden penetration. It certainly did hurt, but not nearly as much as she had expected, somehow. In fact, beyond the discomfort she knew that there was a wonderful new sensation that was only just eluding her. The meaty shaft of his prick pulled out and then rammed back, hard and deep, into her ass, and she gave another scream, softer than the first, more one of surprise and delight; she was definitely beginning to love the feeling of utter helplessness, pinned to the sofa by the weight of his body and the length of his cock like some exotic butterfly transfixed by a pin. And anyway, even if she had wanted it all to stop, there was not a hell of a lot she could have done about it.

"Fuck me, then, goddamn you!" she snarled over her shoulder, and her finger began to fuck in and out of her cunt. She could feel his cock moving inside her ass through the wall of her vagina, and it thrilled her. Ellen stimulated herself harder, and Jim matched her stroke for stroke.

Jim began a steady fucking motion, noticing how her ass now accommodated him far more easily. It never grew less than snug around his prick, but there was no discomfort now that he was fully imbedded, and his fucking became a little gentler, and a lot more exciting.

She continued to masturbate her pussy, his hand joining hers in the effort. While she finger-fucked herself, Jim concentrated on her clit. The pleasurable sensations grew stronger, more difficult to resist. She loved it when he fucked her slow – when he pulled out it was just like she was taking a fantastically enjoyable shit – and she loved it when he fucked hard, like a jackhammer, and made her feel such a sluttish whore. Either way, his prick fucked into her ass again and again, and she chewed her lips, enduring and enjoying this extraordinary, thrilling new sexual experience.

"Oh, you fucker!" she grunted. "Oh, you wonderful, big fucker!"

Ellen loved the way he fucked her asshole. She writhed and swayed, she moaned and whimpered, and then she was coming, coming like some crazy bitch in heat.

She wasn't sure if she was coming in her asshole, her pussy, or both. She only knew that it was the most intense orgasm she had ever experienced.

It seemed to last forever, building into new heights each time she thought it was ebbing. He'd poke her again, deeper, with his driving, ass-pounding cock, and she'd suck in her breath and find herself squealing out a fresh come. Her fingers were dripping as they kept up the pussy attack, and her clit was now so hypersensitive under his fingers that she heard herself begging him to stop.

He stopped frigging her clit and gripped her haunches in his huge hands and started to fuck her ass even harder. It was what she'd asked for, and it was what he gave her.

Suddenly he gasped, and she knew that he was going to come, that he was going to paint her guts with a massive discharge of his jism. She thrust her ass back against him, at the same time squeezing the shaft of his prick tightly with her anal muscles, and she wiggled her hips from side to side, the action giving even more exquisite sensations to the tip of his throbbing cock-head as it started the short countdown to orgasm.

"So – this – is – what – it's – like!" she said gutturally, the words forced out of her by the belly-busting force of Jim Murray's long cock. And even as she spoke, his cock pulsed powerfully within her asshole and began to spurt the first thick load of sperm.

Afterwards they lay on their sides, spooned together, for a long time. Jim's softening penis still hard enough to stay inside her. Every now and then she would flex her anal sphincter and he would reciprocate by squeezing and stroking her lovely, hanging breasts or nuzzling the soft hair at the nape of her neck, which made her shiver gently with pure pleasure. He might be a wild, stormy lover during the act, but after the storm he was somehow so comforting and reassuring. Ellen felt a strong, unfamiliar emotion sweep over her like some great wave. She wanted to weep with relief, with joy, with the tenderness she suddenly felt, she wanted to turn and hide her face in the chest of this gentle giant of a man. But for some reason she held back.

Jim broke the silence.

"You can't stay here, Ellen. Your husband will be back at the apartment in town soon." She nodded in agreement and pulled away from him, feeling the disconnection as his limp cock jerked out of her tender asshole with a little sucking sound. A small rivulet of cum poured out and trickled over the curve of her buttock. She wiped it away with her hand.

* * *

"So, what are you going to do now?" Murray

asked when she had cleaned up in the bathroom and dressed. "You've got the fucker by the balls. Now you've seen what's going on, will you ask for a divorce?"

"I don't know," Ellen said, hooking her bra. "I honestly don't know what I'm going to do. But when I do figure it out, I promise you'll be the first to know."

Chapter 3

When Meredith came home from work, Ellen met him at the door of the duplex apartment. She had called him as soon as she had got back from Jim's place, and now she was freshly washed, powdered, perfumed, and she wore a lush satin robe wrapped around a sheer nightgown. The curves of her body showed through it, and as she kissed him hello, she casually let the robe fall open.

"Hard day, hon?" she asked, stroking his cheek.

Meredith's job with Roeberds was basically a sinecure. He didn't have to exert a muscle or a brain cell to collect his paycheck.

"So-so," he said, easing out of her embrace.

She watched him go past, brushing her

off almost as if she were an embarrassment to him.

He turned at the foot of the stairs.

"Listen, honey, this wasn't the best weekend for a surprise visit," he said, almost apologetically.

Damn right it wasn't, you treacherous asshole, Ellen thought.

"Something's come up and I have to fly to Los Angeles for the weekend. I'm so sorry, I would have let you know in good time, but you know how it is with business. I hope you didn't have a lot planned for us."

Ellen just gave him a long, sardonic stare. Just our divorce, you fuckhead...

Meredith made a show of looking at his watch. "Damn! I'm going to be late for the plane. I'd better grab a shower now. Sorry I can't talk longer, but you know how it is..."

Ellen went up the stairs, listening as he turned on the shower. She went into the bedroom.

She stood by the mirror, examining herself critically in the sheer blue nightgown. She wasn't displeased by what she saw. Maybe not Farrah Fawcett Major or Victoria Principal, but she was damned pretty; she had a decent body: lovely, full breasts and good legs; her belly was flat and she was the proud possessor of a womanly and voluptuous ass. She deserved better than she was getting from her husband.

Ellen opened the bottom drawer of her dresser where she kept her panties and reached into the back. Meredith didn't even know she had a vibrator.

She went to the bed, stretching out across the black satin sheets she'd told the maid to put on. They were smooth and cool against her skin. She felt glamorous and sexy. Too bad her husband didn't appreciate her as much as he should. She couldn't care less. She rolled the sexy black and gold vibrator between her palms, warming it up, and then she switched it on.

She stroked herself with the thing, through her sheer nightgown, arousing her nipples to pointy erections. She squeezed her tit, forcing the nipple to push upward, and the vibrator buzzed fitfully across the tip. A current of sexual electricity seemed to tingle across to the other nipple, then down, all the way down, to her cunt. Ellen began to feel warmer, more excited. Suddenly her cunt was becoming wet. She was starting to feel the way she'd felt at Jim Murray's home. In fact, she couldn't get big Jim Murray out of her mind.

She slid the vibrator down her belly, twisting on the bed as she continued to caress and excite herself. Now her juices were flowing freely, sopping the crotch of her panties, and there was an uncontrollable tingle between her cuntlips, even before she began to work the vibrator back and forth over her clit.

"Ahhhhh!" she gasped, clenching her thighs around the vibrator and pressing it firmly against her sex. She writhed sensually against the satin, clutching her big, hard-nippled breasts. She moved the vibrator against her cunt as if it were a cock, rubbing her aroused pussy until her clit buzzed like a bee and the lips drooled a sticky honey that soaked her panties, her upper thighs and the humming vibrator. She thought of Jim's huge cock.

She eased down the top of her gown, baring her lovely, well-shaped tits. She squeezed them upward to lap at her nipples, lashing them mercilessly with her tongue. By craning her neck forward a little, she was even able to take the entire nipple into her mouth and suck on it greedily. It reminded her of the way Jim Murray had feasted on her tits earlier today, and the memory sent shivers of excitement racing through Ellen's entire body. She bit into the straining flesh of her hardened nipple and her eyes welled with tears of erotic agony.

Down between her thighs, the vibrator was driving her cunt crazy with lust. She kept on sucking at her tit, reaching down with her other hand to grab the vibrator and turn it around. She pressed the point against the crack of her cunt and slid it back and forth, concentrating on the swollen button of clit-flesh.

The shower was still running, and Meredith was singing.

She sat up, pulling the nightgown up over her head and tossing it to the floor. She slid out of the matching panties, flinging them aside too. Stretching across the bed again, she began applying the vibrator directly to her naked body.

Ellen hunched forward and took a tit into her mouth, sucking it with love and lust, while she scraped the vibrator through her dark pussy-hair. The fur was matted with cunt-juice, and her deep pink cunt-lips were swollen and open, as if they were gasping for sex. She slid the tip of the vibrator into the hungry maw of her vaginal cave and thrust, filling her pussy with the solid bulk of the plastic buzz-stick.

She bit into the flesh of her tit once more, sucking away the pain her teeth caused, and she jabbed herself, poking and prodding, moaning at the savage pleasure it gave her. A little like the hard nasty fuck Jim Murray had thrown up her pussy on his living room couch. But she was getting it from plastic and not from flesh, and it wasn't the same thing, not the same thing at all.

"Oh, Christ," she groaned, pulling the vibrator out to use its wet sticky point on her swollen clit. She stretched out, arching upward as she humped the vibrator. Then she hunched once more and pressed her red lips against her aching tits.

That was when Meredith came out of the bathroom.

He was in his short robe, his hair damp, a towel across his shoulder. He stopped short.

She didn't stop, not even to look back at him. She was too deep in her lust by now, and anyway, she wanted him to see that she didn't need him or his cock.

"Hello, darling," she said, her voice husky with almost-fulfilled lust. She gave her wrist a flip and thrust the vibrator back up her cunt, moaning and growling as it penetrated her pussy once again. Her cunt sucked wildly at the buzzing dildo, holding it so possessively she found it difficult to fuck the thing in and out of herself.

She was glowing now, she knew, as wet from sweat as Meredith had gotten from his shower. She could smell her funky pussy scent, and it was intoxicating.

She'd never masturbated in front of Meredith before. He stared in fascination, seeing a brand new side of his wife.

Meredith took a step closer to the bed. Ellen sneaked a look at him through half-closed eyes. The front of his robe was beginning to tent out, and she knew what was responsible.

She swivelled around, presenting her engorged, wet cunt to his staring eyes. She knew exactly what she was doing. Now he could see the vibrator fucking in and out of her, see the labia spreading to make room for it, see the wetness that coated the black plastic shaft as it emerged. She was fucking her cunt toward the vibrator, eating it greedily, and her clit was enormously swollen, gleaming like a pearl above her splayed pussy-lips. She reached down to frig her clit and Meredith came nearer to the bed.

His robe slipped open, and his stiff prick pushed outward. He had a perfectly nice cock, she had to admit, smaller than Jim's but a nice one, one she'd grown to love since they'd been together. She'd certainly excited him with her display, and it gave her a tingle of satisfied pleasure.

"This is so... unlike you, darling," he said.

He sat down on the bed beside her, stroking her soft hair and shoulders while she fucked herself with the vibrator. She bit her lip and concentrated on herself.

He took her free hand and put it on his stiff prick. She let her hand be guided, let her fingers be moulded around his hard cock, but her hand was limp and loose. He squeezed the fingers down, until they clutched him. She felt the hot pulsation of lust inside his cock.

"Do me too... play with my cock!" he whispered, and he guided her hand up and down, moving his cock inside it.

She was in no mood to cooperate with him. But she allowed her hand to be used, and she kept on fucking herself with her hot, battery-powered vibrator.

The harder she fucked herself with the dildo, though, the more tightly her other hand gripped Meredith's cock. His hands were all over her.

"You look so wild and hot," he said. "I can't believe you're doing this. It's not like you at all – mmmmm, lean over here and kiss my cock, will you, darling?"

Ellen resisted his efforts to push her face down toward his cock, and she continued to assault her pussy with the plastic prick.

But he seemed to be determined to get his cock into her mouth, and he pried her fingers loose, then brushed the head of his cock against Ellen's cheek. She felt the velvety sponginess slide across her flesh, drizzling a thread of clear pre-cum as it touched her.

The dildo was pounding in and out of her cunt, emerging from time to time to buzz her clit again, then slamming deep and hard into her fuck-hole once more. She felt her face being turned toward Meredith's cock, and she relaxed, allowing him to do what he wanted.

His prick touched her mouth, and the

old familiar scent of him filled her nostrils. She sniffed, then opened up, and he thrust between her lips.

There was a certain pleasure in sucking his prick, and she rationalized that after all, he had taken a bath and washed himself since he'd been with that red-haired cunt. She probably couldn't catch anything serious from a little nibble on his dick. And God, she did still so love to suck him! But wait, she thought, the cock she was taking into her mouth had been in that slut's filthy ass! But perversely, that obscene thought only spurred her on to taking his manhood between her lips.

Her mouth grew wet and slurping on Meredith's cock, and he was fondling her tits and reaching low down her belly to frig her clit while she continued to fuck the dildo. He spread her cunt-lips wide, and then squeezed them tightly around the dildo, increasing the pressure and the stimulation all at once.

He spread her wide again, and his finger slicked into her cunt, probing alongside the burrowing shaft of the dildo. She got very wet around him. She found herself jerking wildly with lustful responses. Her sucking grew more determined, more intense.

His cock had become almost too big for Ellen to suck properly, but she knew she was doing a damn good job anyway. He thrust across her lapping tongue, his rubbery glans pulsing into the upper end of her throat. She gagged a little but kept on gobbling.

He pulled her upper body around and started fucking deeper and faster into her mouth.

"You're acting just like some sort of whore," he said slowly, "and, hell, I think I like it!"

Now she was on her knees, her head buried in his lap, her ass in the air, the dildo humming away as it protruded from Ellen's dripping pussy. She had both hands on Meredith's cock as she fed it in and out of her mouth. He reached beneath her and started to manipulate the vibrator, fucking her with it in short but passionate thrusts. He even slipped it out, as she had done, and buzzed her clit, but he gave her a couple of gooses up the ass with the thing, too!

He knew she didn't go for any of that asshole stuff! But she couldn't help thinking of what she had forced Jim Murray to do to her today, and each time the vibrator's tip tingled outside her shit-hole, she felt a fresh dribble of pussy-juice trickle down her quivering, sweat-soaked thighs.

She climaxed. The come ripped through her like a chainsaw and she howled around the cock that fucked her wet mouth. The humming sound set off a chain reaction in Meredith's cock, and suddenly she felt soft jets of his cum in her mouth; she let her mouth go slack and the white cum dripped thickly down the shaft of his detumescent penis, matting his pubic bush and coating his balls.

"So," she said, lying smug and contented with her head in his lap and his cum dripping from her chin, "do you really have to go to LA?"

"Oh, shit!" he gasped. "I almost forgot about that! I'm going to be late. Listen, Ellen, this is major, and I can't get out of it. And when duty calls – you know?"

I know, Ellen thought. But it's not duty that's calling you. It's a red-haired cunt called Nancy McGuinness.

She sat up.

"Okay," she said grimly. "If you have to, you have to."

If he noticed the icy tone of her voice, Meredith gave no indication of it. "I'd better take another shower," he said. "I seem to smell like I've just gotten fucked." He leaned down and kissed Ellen on her cum-smeared lips. "We'll have to try this again when I come home. Where in hell did you ever get that dildo, dearest? It doesn't seem your style at all. I like it, but it just doesn't seem your style."

And with that he went back into the bathroom.

Ellen lay on the bed, staring after him with a mixture of lust and revulsion.

"All right, you fucker," Ellen said, once she heard the shower water running and the sound of his singing, "if you don't want it, let's find out if anyone else does."

Chapter 4

"You don't want any money?" the man asked. "This isn't some kind of weird scam?"

Ellen Fielding smiled. "No, it isn't some kind of weird scam. I simply feel like being fucked tonight, and I thought maybe you were the man to do it. If you're not, I can always look for someone else."

She stood up, putting down her drink. She was wearing a red dress, tight in the bodice to show off her tits, low-cut into the cleavage, and ending short to show off her long, black-stockinged legs.

"Well?" she asked.

"Don't go," he said, putting down his own drink. Gingerly, still uncertain, he came near. Ellen smiled and waited.

She had picked him up in the lounge of the hotel where he was staying. Last night she had confirmed that Mr. and Mrs. Fielding had boarded a flight to Los Angeles. She had spent the day feeling sorry for herself, but by the evening she was ready for some payback, big time.

That had been the clincher. If Meredith could go to LA with his slut, then Ellen had no qualms about going on the prowl. The Satin Lounge was the top pick-up spot in town. Ellen had scored not five minutes through the door, and now they were in his hotel room.

The man was a salesman, leaving town in the morning. He was gorgeous, the kind of big blond stud Ellen had always dreamed about in her school days, though she always froze up around them in real life. His name was Tim.

He put his hands on her waist and she leaned in to him, brushing her tits against his chest. Her nipples were hard through the soft clinging fabric of her dress. He couldn't help but feel them touching him. She pushed a little more firmly, making sure he felt them. His hands moved around her waist and down onto the curves of her ass.

She squeezed closer, her belly starting to grind against his crotch.

She kissed him hungrily, her mouth wet and open. Her eagerness seemed to scare him a little, but the more she fucked her tongue in and out of his mouth, the more excited he grew. His hands cupped her asscheeks, squeezing them possessively, and now he was grinding back at her, and his prick was beginning to show some definite signs of interest.

Ellen came up for air, licking her lips and smiling. She had her arms around his neck. She swayed, her asscheeks swaying too inside his cupping hands. She felt the surging energy as it flowed into his cock, stiffening him against her.

"I'm for real," she said huskily, "but are you?"

He didn't say anything. She wriggled out of his grasp and took a couple of steps back, wobbling a bit on the heels. Turning, she looked over her shoulder and said, "Would you unzip me, please, Tim?"

He tugged down the zipper of her dress. She leaned forward, easing it off her shoulders and down her body. It fell to her ankles, and she stepped out of it. Under the dress she wore a pink teddy, its front laces undone, with black stockings and bright red shoes. She was sure that she looked good, and his eyes confirmed her suspicions.

"God," he said, staring into the front of her teddy. The undone laces showed tantalizing glimpses of the curves of her tits, and the nipples protruded insistently under the smooth silk.

"Touch them, if you want," she said, taking his hands and placing them on her tits. She forced his fingers downward. "Would you like to see them?"

He nodded, and she slid the straps of the teddy off her shoulders. It fell to her waist, where she caught it, and she confronted him with her tits, bare and tempting.

"Your body is gorgeous," Tim whispered, his eyes alive with lust.

"Now you take something off," she said. "I bet you have a beautiful body, too."

He did. She had to restrain a gulp as he got out of his clothes. His shoulders were broad, his chest smooth and hard-looking, his waist tapering and narrow. He removed his pants, stumbling slightly, but her eyes were on his crotch, not his feet. He wore a pair of tight bikini shorts. The lance-like shaft of his cock was protruding above the low-riding top of the shorts.

His cock was long – not overly thick, but really long – and Ellen eyed him, her mouth watering for the taste of his cock.

She dropped her teddy, leaving her naked except for stockings. Her eyebrows lifted, and Tim yanked down his shorts. His cock jumped out, long and hard and ready for love.

She took it in her fists, sliding them up and down the length of Tim's cock. He was almost long enough that she needed both hands to masturbate him properly. As it was, she could wrap two fists around his cock and there was still a little bit peeking out of her handhold. Leaning toward him, she pressed her tits – bare now, the nipples hot and stiff – against his chest.

He took her head in his hands and kissed her savagely.

"I don't even know your name," he said, breaking free.

"It's Dana," she said, lying. What business of his was her name, anyway? The only thing that mattered between them was the swollen, raging prick she clutched in her fists. The only thing.

They moved to the bed. He picked her up like a bridegroom and carried her over, depositing her carefully on the mattress. She looked up at him, stroking her tits and pinching the nipples even harder. They were dark red, suffused with lust, and her eyes flashed fire.

He knelt by the bed, leaning across her where she lay. He started at her mouth and kissed his way down to her engorged nipples. She moaned in gratification as he took them in his mouth, one after the other. He squeezed her tits together and sucked his way back and forth, munching, biting, licking, and fed the pointy-capped mounds into his mouth for hungry swallows of Ellen's soft, pliant flesh.

One hand, meanwhile, was down between her legs. He slid his fingers up and down the soft, hairy bulge of her cunt, stretching the meaty cunt-lips, opening them, then squashing them shut again. She writhed responsively, her hands all over him, urging him to do more.

"You really do want it, don't you?" he said softly. "You're dripping wet!"

His finger moved through the deep pink inner lips of her cunt, tickling the wet, aroused opening. She gasped and started as he jabbed her fuck-hole with little ceremony, and then plunged into her, his finger burying itself in the hot, tight wetness. Her body bucked and trembled as he began to finger-fuck her pussy and suck at her aroused tits in earnest. Rough treatment from a stranger's hand, she thought, and I just love it.

He moved his lips down her belly. He was finding spots she hadn't even guessed were responsive, but which came alive at the touch of his mouth, his tongue. His hand manipulated her cunt in a smooth, knowing fashion, and her juices puddled in his palm.

"Eat my cunt!" she whispered. "Get me hot!"

"Kerrist, honey, you were fuckin' born hot," he laughed softly, his mouth easing into the upper edge of her pussy-bush.

He licked down toward her cunt, opening her cunt-lips until her clit stood out.

"Oh Jeez!" Ellen gasped as he tongued her back and forth, inching slowly toward the rising button of her clit. His finger poked back into her cunt.

She reached down and found his cock. It was as hard and long as before. She stroked it vigorously while he licked her cunt.

His tongue came down onto her clit, finally, and she almost screamed at its touch, lapping the tingly hard button. His finger was deep inside her cunt, and she squirmed, writhed, and fucked back on his finger with a ravenous pussy.

"Oh, now, please eat me, eat me!" she moaned from low in her throat. "Eat my fucking pussy!"

He spread the cunt-lips wide and thrust his face up into Ellen's hot horny cunt-gash, breathing in the heady scent of her arousal, his tongue stabbing ahead of him to enter her as deep as he could lick.

He wiggled into her, and his tongue licked her inside out, reaming softly but provocatively around her pussy. She lifted her ass straight off the bed and she came all over his sucking mouth.

She still had a fistful of his prick, and the saliva in her mouth told Ellen that it was time to do some sucking of her own.

"Get up on the bed!" she panted. "Let me eat that cock before I die!"

He quickly did as she asked and she spun around instantly, making for the rigid pole of his prick. She took it in both hands, marveling at the length and stiffness.

He had thighs like granite. She couldn't get over how firm and muscular they were. She wanted to keep on fondling his prick or caress the perfection of his upper legs. His stomach was flat and hard, too, and she stroked her palm across it.

He had little body hair, other than what grew in his armpits and around his proud cock. Ellen slid her hand up his thigh again, and over onto the long pole of his prick, then leaned in to suck him blind.

She extended her tongue and tickled the edges of his bell-shaped cock head with it. He shivered in her grip, and she smiled. Men really loved to have their cocks licked, and Tim was no exception.

"Dana, baby!"

She'd almost forgotten what name she had given him.

She made her licking a little more aggressive, relishing his clean male scent and taste. She coated his cockhead with saliva.

She traced the bulging shape of his cock straight down to his balls. She pushed his balls aside and licked the area beneath his scrotal bag, down toward his asshole.

"Kerr-ist, you're a dirty bitch, Dana," he said appreciatively, patting her head. "C'mon, now lick my ass, too!"

She rolled him over, gave his ass a playful nip with her teeth, then spread his hard, muscular asscheeks wide, sliding her tongue tentatively up and down the crack.

His shitter was tiny, but it dilated when she pried his asscheeks open, and she almost grinned at the way it seemed to wink back at her. Satisfying herself that he was perfectly clean she leant down and flicked it with her tongue, rimming the wrinkly flesh, poking into it as if she meant to fuck him orally in the ass.

"Oh, that hits the spot," he said, but by then she was tonguing her way down to his balls, attacking them from behind.

She reached under Tim and grabbed his cock, stroking it with a growing eagerness while she kept on licking and sucking everything that wasn't nailed down.

She got a mouthful of balls, humming as she sucked them.

Then he turned over, and she began to devour his cock with hungry lips, gulping him in. She couldn't get even half of his long cock into her mouth, so she sucked and licked all she could, running her tongue up and down the stiff tube of flesh, her saliva wetting its entire length.

She came back up, concentrating on the knob of his prick, and she feasted on the firm, spongy head while her busy fingers stroked and jerked the rest of him. He was reaching for her, and she squirmed around, opening her cunt to his fingers. He speared three fingers up her pussy-hole, fucking Ellen while she sucked his cock. It was pretty clear he liked what he was getting. And he wasn't the only one.

Ellen's face lifted and she said, "Well, lover, are you going to fuck me or not?" He grabbed her by the waist and spread her on the bed. Her legs spread automatically and she reached down to spread her pussy for him. He came down on his knees, between her thighs, and she caught his cock in her other hand, bringing it to bear against her drooling cunt-crack.

She moved his penis head in and out of her pussy, teasing herself with the promise of a full insertion till she could hardly stand it.

"Now!" she cried. "Fuck me right now!"

He nodded and thrust, and she got her fingers out of the way just before the power of his thrust would have buried them alongside his prick in her pussy.

"How's this?" he gasped, burying his prick in her ready cunt. His belly slammed against hers, and the sparse hairs he had were in exactly the right position to rub against her clit. She opened her mouth to shriek, but no sounds came out.

Tim was propped above her, supported by

his arms and knees. He was stirring her cunt with his long cock, and she tossed her head from side to side, biting her lip and murmuring.

She couldn't remember ever having been penetrated quite so deeply. She couldn't remember ever having been more excited by being penetrated.

"Fuck me, goddamn you!" she growled beneath him, grinding her hips and milking his cock in and out of her spasmodically convulsing pussy. "Now! Now, oh now, now!"

He got the message, and he started to fuck her hard and deep, showing her cunt no mercy with his long prick. It banged to the bottom of her pussy, hitting hard, and she made a high, animalistic keening sound with each stroke he gave. Her feet kicked up into the air. She alternately spread and squeezed her legs, trying to vary the tightness of her cunt around his cock and drawing an increasing pleasure from the sensation of being fucked.

It was just too much for Tim who gasped, and his prick began to unload inside Ellen in a series of violent spurts.

"Dana, baby!" he gasped, as her cunt started to fill with his gooey cum.

He continued to fuck into the sticky mess, and it oozed out of her cunt each time he thrust home to give her another squirt, making an obscene sloshing sound. She was moaning and climaxing, her legs wrapped around his thighs and her hands clawing at his chest as she urged him to give her more.

He pulled his dripping cock out of her pussy and crawled up her chest, his dripping prick protruding before him. She took it in her hands, relishing the sticky feel of cum that coated his cock, and she fed it into her mouth, sucking hard at the dribble of whitish sperm that continued to escape from the piss slit in his cockhead.

*　*　*

"Why were you so hesitant?" she asked as they shared a shower, soaping each other. "Were you afraid of me?"

"Jeez, Dana," he said, shaking his head, "a guy in my position has to be careful. I can't just fuck anything that looks good while I'm on the road. You're a total doll, sure, but there are some girls around who aren't as neat and clean as you. I'm a married man, and my wife would kill me if I came home with a dose of something nasty."

"You're married?" she said, stiffening. Ellen ignored the naivety of his comments about sexual diseases. She knew quite well that cleanliness was no guarantee of sexual health. But somehow the knowledge of Tim's betrayed wife changed the whole complexion of things. "Why didn't you say so?"

"Hey, doll, my wife is a long way from here, and what she doesn't know can't ever hurt her, right?"

Ellen brushed past him, out of the shower, not bothering to answer. She dried herself quickly and started to dress.

"Thanks for a great fuck," she said softly and without even much irony as she picked up her purse. "I'd say let's do it again sometime, but I don't screw married men..." But Tim couldn't hear her. He was still in the shower as she closed the door of the room behind her.

Downstairs, back at the bar, she tossed down a drink. Shit, I'm no better than that bitch Nancy McGuinness, she thought.

*   *   *

While she sat at the long bar a couple of men tried to hit on her, but she was no longer in the mood for male company. She ordered a second drink, took a sip, and a hand brushed her shoulder. She turned and found herself looking directly into the almond-eyed, quizzical gaze of a tall, devastatingly pretty Oriental girl. Chinese, maybe mixed race. She couldn't be sure. Straight, shining black hair down to the small of her back; in front it was cut in a fringe that nearly covered her saucy, arched eyebrows and framed her very cute features: big brown eyes, a tiny button nose and big, luscious lips. She was most likely in her thirties, though Ellen.

"You wanna make quick hundred?" the girl asked in a slightly singsong voice, her imperfect use of English suggesting that she was an only recently naturalized American. "Me in big trouble. Could really use help. You help me?"

Chapter 5

She thinks I'm a hooker! Ellen realized, a few sentences into the conversation. She blushed, but the darkness hid her embarrassment, and the Oriental didn't notice.

"He easy trick," she said. "I got john upstairs who want two girls, and that rotten bitch Daisy do fucking vanishing trick on me. She supposed to help me, but I no find her. She probably blow somebody's dog for small change. She such a cunt!"

"But you nice. You very nice…"

She smiled and ran her fingers up and down Ellen's bare arm.

"Oh, c'mon, babe, you see, it no problem. Easy hundred dollar! You just watch while he fuck me. He like audience, but only girl audience. You do it? My old man beat shit outta me if I come home no cash. You save my ass. Trick worth three hundred, you get hundred just for watching. You say yes, honey, please?"

Intrigued and strangely attracted to this beautiful, exotic girl, Ellen was unable to resist. She nodded quickly. The girl grinned and said, "You call me Suzie. You come with me. Have good time. You no be sorry!"

* * *

In the suite, Suzie was snuggling up to a balding guy in his forties. His beer belly bulged out of his T-shirt and a big wad showed inside his shorts. All the same, he wasn't unattractive, Ellen thought. Probably another out-of-towner, with a wife at home who had no idea what kind of stuff her husband was up to on the road.

Suzie stood up and the guy unzipped her skin-tight dress, peeling it down her body. Underneath she wore a black bra and panties. The bra pushed her tits upward, making the most of their rather small size. Her skin was pale, as if she hadn't seen the sun in years, and the black garments were eye-catching against her milky complexion.

The guy – his name was Marlon – moved against her from behind, grinding his crotch into her pert little ass, his hands coming around to cup and squeeze her apple-sized tits.

"Great as ever, Suzie," he said. Looking over at Ellen, he added, "Why don't you get comfortable too?"

Ellen stood up, watching the man fondle Suzie. *All I have to do is watch,* she reminded herself. *And it might be fun. I've never watched another couple fucking – except my husband and that cunt Nancy,* she reminded herself bitterly. She unzipped her dress and stepped out of it. Marlon's eyebrows lifted at the sight of Ellen in her teddy and stockings, and he smiled.

"Not bad, baby. Maybe we'll make this a threesome."

Suzie unsnapped her bra and peeled it loose. Her tits were small but high and firm, with light brown areolas and bud-like nipples that pointed upward at a perky angle. She tweaked them, rolling them between finger and thumb, then cupped her tits and offered them to Marlon. She craned her neck and began licking at them with a long, pink tongue.

Ellen pulled up a chair and sat down, her legs open. One of the shoulder straps of her teddy came down, and the edge of a stiffening nipple teasingly peeked in and out around it. She felt a little strange being in this position, but then these days she was beginning to feel pretty good about strange feelings.

As she watched Marlon sucking on Suzie's tit, she eased her teddy down and bared one of her tits completely. Her hand brushed across the nipple point and she felt it growing harder, hotter. She reversed her hand and squeezed at her tit, bringing her thighs together so that they pressed against the swelling cleft of her pussy.

Marlon straightened up. His belly was a little on the large side but Ellen didn't find it all that unsexy. On the contrary, she was beginning to appreciate all the different varieties of male physique. Especially when she glanced down and saw the size of the cock-bulge in his shorts.

Suzie stole a glance at Ellen, giving her a conspiratorial wink. She turned to Marlon and thrust a slim hand into his shorts, taking hold of his fast-growing prick and gently shaking it.

"Mmmmmm, honey," she said in a silky, throaty voice, "you got hell of a cock! You want stick that thing in me? Fucky-fucky?"

"Mmmm-hmmm, fucky-fucky," said Marlon, his hands busy on her springy tits. "That's exactly what I planned on doing!"

Suzie giggled and dropped to her knees, pulled his shorts down, and his prick swung outward. Ellen was more than slightly impressed. It was perhaps the thickest cock she'd ever seen, tapering to a sharp-looking prick-head. It reminded her of a railroad spike.

"Nice prick!" Suzie sighed, stroking it with her long slim fingers. "Me think maybe I suck it, just little bit."

Sucking it was clearly on her mind, but first she licked every inch of Marlon's cock, her tongue gliding wetly across the flesh. Ellen had no idea what it was like to have a prick, but as she watched, she imagined that she could feel every lick Suzie dished out, feel that wet tongue sliding over her own flesh. It was a crazy feeling. She squeezed harder at her tit, and her other hand began to slide up and down the inside of her thigh, between the edge of her teddy and the top of her stocking. She was very sensitive there, and her flesh began to tingle.

"Watch her," Marlon said hoarsely. "Watch her while I fuck her red-lipped mouth!"

He grabbed two great fistfuls of Suzie's soft black hair, either side of her head, and shoved his cock into her open, willing mouth. She gulped and gasped as he pushed in and out. He was a little rough, and more than a little eager, and his long cock fucked the almond-eyed whore's mouth with a growing energy. It was nothing that Suzie couldn't handle. She gagged a little when he fucked deep, her delicate features screwing up in a brief grimace, but quickly recovered and kept on bravely sucking and licking, her hands moving up and down his chest, his belly, under the T-shirt.

Marlon not the most handsome guy Ellen had ever seen. In real life she wouldn't have given him a second look, but this wasn't real life, not tonight. And besides, there was something undeniably sexy about him in this context. Tonight she was walking on the wild side and all the old rules were off.

She took down the other side of her teddy, and now both tits were bare. She cupped them, making a mock offering of her tits to Marlon. He was too busy, by far, fucking Suzie's mouth, to take her up on the invitation. Ellen just smiled and continued to play with her tits while she watched him fucking her new girlfriend in the mouth.

"Are you getting excited, watching me shove my cock in her mouth?" Marlon asked, still holding Suzie's head as he slowly thrust into her mouth with his cock. He was deep throating her, Ellen realised with a sudden shock. The Chinese hooker made a purry rattling noise, as if she were gargling, as he thrust into her, so deep now that his balls were jiggling against her chin.

"Is this making you hot?"

"It is, oh yes, it is!" Ellen gasped.

She leaned forward to lick at her nearest nipple, her tongue fluttering across the stiffened pink point. She pressed her red-painted lips to the flesh of her tit and left a big round smear of lipstick.

Marlon was watching her now, and she made a sexy production of it, slipping the end of her tit into her mouth and sucking at the nipple.

She pulled the crotch of her teddy out of the way and exposed her hairy cunt to Marlon's eyes. He smiled in approval, and she began to openly frig herself while he watched, her fingers stroking intensely up and down the crack of her pussy. The damp cunt-lips opened, and if he couldn't see the pink, he needed an urgent visit to the oculist.

"Oh, yes!" Ellen moaned, sliding the tip of her middle finger into her cunt.

She worked it in and out until she was wet, and then she began to caress her hardening clit with the tip of the pussy-wet finger. Closing her eyes, she purred in response, momentarily thinking only of herself.

But she could hear the greedy sucking sounds that Suzie made, and she had to look again. Her big eyes opened wide.

"Get up here, bitch!" Marlon growled as he pulled Suzie to her feet.

The slim Oriental sucked his tongue, just like she'd sucked his cock, and he ran his hands up and down her long, lithe body.

"Now it's my turn," he said, pushing her facedown onto the bed. Her legs hung over the side, and he pulled down her panties, and then spread her thighs, stooping between them.

Suzie's cunt was hairless. It reminded Ellen of a bread roll, only the furrow was in the shape of a long pink cleft. It looked soft as velvet and sweet as honey. Ellen pushed her finger more deeply into her own pussy as she stared with burning curiosity at Marlon and Suzie.

The middle-aged man dropped to his knees now, pushing his face into Suzie's crotch. He was just as noisy eating cunt as the Oriental had been while sucking his prick. Ellen thought his attack a little more aggressive and less refined than she would have preferred for herself, but it was certainly fascinating to watch other people doing it. She'd never seen anything like it before, and it was making her hotter than she would have thought possible.

Marlon kept on slurping Suzie's pussy, shoving his face up into it. He spread her tight little buns and licked swiftly up and down, from the dark brown pucker of her shit-hole to her clit. She made squealing sounds that were too sharp to be anything but honest responses. It struck Ellen for the very first time that a whore might actually get off on her work.

The man looked over his shoulder at Ellen, smiling in approval when he saw the way she was playing with herself.

"Why don't you tickle yourself with a vibrator?" he said. "The buzzing always makes my cock hard as steel."

"I don't have one," Ellen said, finger-fucking her pussy.

"Mine in purse," Suzie said, nodding her head in the direction of where she had placed her purse.

Ellen reached into the girl's purse and sure enough, she was carrying a vibrator there. It looked a lot like the dildo Ellen used on herself at home. She switched the thing on and began to stroke herself with it – first her tits, then her belly, then her pussy.

She leaned back in the chair, stretching her legs out as she worked on her cunt with the vibrator. Holding the crotch of her teddy to the side, she slid the point up and down the crease of her pussy, nosing it in until her cunt-hole opened and gulped hungrily at the dildo's tip.

Marlon was still eating out Suzie. She writhed across the surface of the bed, alternately pulling her cunt away from his mouth and then thrusting it to meet him.

Ellen couldn't help noticing that the man was also licking and rimming Suzie's asshole. He dug his fingers into the luxurious sponginess of her asscheeks, spreading them wide and making the hole pop open. His tongue tickled around and around the dilated opening, screwing into it while Suzie cooed and sighed with obvious pleasure.

"Gonna let me fuck you up the ass tonight baby?" Marlon asked between slurps. "Gonna let me stick that cock up your tight shit-hole?"

"You know I no take you up asshole!" Suzie said, sounding just a little admonitory. "You just too thick! You rip Suzie wide open! I only let little dicks bang asshole, your cock too big! You fuck in cunt, like always!"

She rolled over, spreading her legs wide and reaching down to split her cunt-gash wider still. She was as pink and pretty as a carnation inside, and a glaze of moisture gave sheen and glisten to her shamelessly displayed sex.

"Why you no put your big cock right here in pussy, honey?" she asked, pointing animatedly to her deliciously wet gash. "You fuck my pussy. Then you no have time to worry about asshole!"

Marlon stood up, peeling off his T-shirt. He was big, and he was hairy, too. Ellen knew, even without touching it, that his big belly was hard, not flabby, and she found herself aching to slide her sensitized fingers through the dark hair that covered much of his torso.

She had an inch of dildo up her cunt now,

the vibrator's tip buzzing wickedly inside her. She rotated it, accentuating the pleasure that filled her pussy alongside the inserted dildo. The buzzing stimulation prodded her clit from beneath. Wetness was oozing out of her fuck-hole. She could feel it trickling down the shaft of the dildo, toward the clutching fingers that guided the cock surrogate in and out of her excited cunt.

Marlon climbed onto the bed. Suzie lifted her knees as his body mounted hers, and she reached down to guide his cock into her cunt. Now it seemed far too big for her delicate little slit. But evidently the slim Chinese girl thought otherwise and bucked her hips upwards to meet his thrust.

"Oh, yeah, you fuck me good now!" she gasped as his prick sank into her.

The big man pushed hard, ramming his groin onto hers, and Suzie moaned in pleasure beneath him. Her legs enfolded his body and she bucked and fucked, shoving herself up to meet his descending strokes of penetration.

Ellen watched in total fascination. She could see the hard, juice-slick length of cock that joined Marlon's body to Suzie's, see it in motion, like the bit of a drill shoving repeatedly into the Chinese girl's velvety pussy. Marlon strained and gasped as he fucked.

Ellen shoved the dildo into her pussy, mimicking what she saw Marlon do to Suzie.

She stood up, still fucking herself, and walked stiff-legged to the bed, weaving a little in her ungainly high heels. She wanted a closer look. She wanted to do more than just look!

Her legs tight together, the vibrator shoved halfway up her pussy and held it position by her muscular control, she leaned forward and rubbed both palms up and down Marlon's back. She caressed him as he worked his cock again and again into the whore's cunt, and her excitement grew tremendously.

Her hands moved down to his ass. She squeezed down hard, her fingers gripping his solid, muscular buns, feeling them flex as he fucked Suzie's pussy. She could feel the tension, the exertion and the passionate arousal that controlled his fucking. Carefully, she cupped his balls, squeezing a little on them.

It seemed to be a good natural instinct.

"Oh, shit, yes, baby!"

His fucking grew harder, more energetic. The bed creaked and rocked beneath Suzie and her john. The slim, black-haired girl moaned and sighed, and her hands were down on Marlon's ass, too, the fingers stroking Ellen's as they played over Marlon firm, rippling flesh.

There was something really exciting about all of it. She was touching, and being touched, by people who were engaged in an act of fucking that she was not a part of. She leaned closer, pressing her lovely bare tits against Marlon's hairy shoulders.

Her hot nipples scraped his skin. She felt him respond as if he had been scalded. His cock fucked harder into Suzie. The Oriental moaned and whimpered beneath the big man, her legs sawing around his body as her delicate-looking pussy took stab after stab from his rampant, lustful cock.

Ellen slid her hand down, past his balls, so that it was between his cock and Suzie's velvety cunt. She squeezed it, locking her fingers around the base of his prick so that he had to fuck his way through the tight ring of finger and thumb as he thrust repeatedly into Suzie's vaginal tunnel. Ellen clenched her thighs, pressing the vibrator a little deeper into her own pussy, and she felt weak in the knees, giddy in the head and horny in the cunt, all at the same time.

Suzie's hand was creeping up Ellen's arm. The adventurous married woman hardly noticed, until she felt the fingers slide delicately onto the swell of her right tit, making for the pink peak of her erect nipple. Ellen closed her eyes, gasping in a mixture of shock and delight.

No woman had never touched her so intimately before. Maybe I'm half a Lesbian, she wondered, idly. Suzie's hand closed around Ellen's tit, and it pulsated excitedly, the nipple stiffening even more against the woman's damp palm. Suzie rubbed her hand briskly, and Ellen began to shudder and throb responsively.

She reached around, past Marlon, and her hand touched Suzie. She was slick with sweat, though whether it was hers or Marlon's was not certain. In any case her firm skin was slippery and Ellen's hand simply skidded onto one of Suzie's small tits, and she closed down, the way Suzie had taken possession of her own tit.

She marvelled at the firmness of Suzie's round tit. It was small but supple, and the rubbery nipple throbbed in her palm as she squeezed it. She thought she could feel heat rising through the pores of the woman's flesh.

Suzie leaned forward and kissed Ellen's upper arm, her lips wet and greedy.

Marlon turned his head. He caught Ellen by surprise, pressing his mouth against hers. She attempted to speak, but he was already in control, and his tongue wiggled wetly into her open mouth. She knew that the curious taste coating his tongue had come from Suzie's pussy, and she was pleased to discover that it wasn't a nasty taste at all.

"I know you're just here to watch," the man said, "but what the fuck, baby, why don't you join us? Make it a threesome? I'll spot you an extra hundred if you're willing." He put his arm around her waist and kissed her again. "What do you say?"

"I say make it an extra two and you've got a deal," said Ellen dryly. Not my dad's daughter for nothing she thought, smiling secretly to herself.

Chapter 6

"You come here," Suzie said, her arm encircling Ellen. She turned Ellen's face towards her. Her mouth drew near Ellen's, her breath warm and sweet, and her lips pressed firmly, wetly, against those of her new friend. "We do it together!"

Ellen climbed onto the bed, reminding herself that she had set out as a sexual adventuress this evening. Why stop now? She'd already given herself to a stranger. Would another one hurt?

Marlon slid off Suzie, his long stiff prick popping out of her cunt. Ellen's eyes enlarged at the sight of it, coated in wet pussy-drippings.

"I help you get naked," Suzie said, assisting Ellen out of her teddy. She'd already done a lot of teasing exposure, but it felt fresh and kinky to be totally nude with this pair of strangers. She basked in the appreciation of their eyes, of their hands.

Ellen lay back, her knees up, her body totally exposed, and Marlon removed the vibrator from her cunt.

Suzie leaned down to kiss her again, her hands covering Ellen's bare, pointy-nippled tits, and Ellen sighed to receive that kiss, her mouth opening to allow Suzie's tongue a little exploratory space. She wasn't sure what kind of things whores did to other women, but she expected she was going to find out pretty soon.

Marlon moved Suzie's fingers aside, allowing a nipple point to swell lusciously between them. He tweaked it hard, making Ellen giggle and whimper, and then he bent down to lap it with his tongue, taking away all the momentary hurt. Ellen surrendered herself to Marlon and Suzie. Whatever they wanted, she was sure she could provide.

Both of them stroked her bare body. Marlon's hand cupped her cunt, squeezed it, and when he moved away, she felt the ticklish touch of Suzie's fingers moving through her pussy-hair. From the corner of her eyes, she glanced at Suzie's cunt, wondering what it would be like to feel a hairless pussy.

There was no apparent game plan from that point onward. What happened simply happened.

Ellen stroked her finger along the wet crack of Suzie's cunt, marvelling at the velvety softness of her outer labia, the slickness of the coral-pink inner lips that furled, then unfurled as her fingers sluiced through them. Suzie held her wrist, guiding the hand.

"Yes, you fucky your finger in me!" she moaned, straightening out the middle finger of Ellen's hand and easing it into the already-fucked opening of her cunt.

She was like warm jelly inside, the lining of her pussy awash in sticky fuck-juices. Ellen knew what it was like to finger-fuck her own cunt, she just hadn't ever realized that other women's pussies felt very much like her own, once they were horny and hot and something nice was inside them.

Her finger began to move in and out, mimicking the stabs of a fuck-thirsty cock, and she felt Suzie move in response, her flat belly undulating, her cunt rippling up and down the length of the inserted finger. Her hand ground against the mouth of Suzie's cuntgash, and she felt the stubby button of Suzie's clit throbbing each time she touched it.

Just the way her own clit was throbbing, as Marlon pressed her from behind. His hands caressed her big, hard-nippled tits, and the length of his cock was shoved between her legs, its shaft masturbating the exterior of Ellen's pussy. It slid aggressively through her cunt-bush and along the crack of her cunt.

Ellen squeezed her thighs around the stiffness, trapping it. She moved in jerky little responses, bobbing up and down. She could feel the prick growing bigger and bigger within the grip of her thighs, and she couldn't help wondering how much larger it might grow once she'd taken it up her pussy for some serious fucking.

Suzie wanted more kisses, and Ellen found herself growing happier and happier to give them. Their tongues fought back and forth, dribbling spit from one mouth to the other, and their lips were as wet as the inside of Suzie's cunt. Ellen's finger pushed in and out, piercing the eager-to-be-fucked tube of muscle, pushing as deep into the other woman's cunt as she could thrust.

It was a relatively snug pussy – surprisingly so, considering that Suzie was a pro. Ellen had expected a cunt as wide as a barn door.

Marlon mauled her tits with his hands. He couldn't get enough of the feel of her big tits, and he milked the nipples until they seemed three or four inches long, his fingers savagely tweaking the delicate but resilient peaks. And his cock throbbed, lustfully, wickedly between her clutching thighs, its firm back-and-forth thrusts making fresh bubbles of juice ooze from Ellen's lusty cunt.

She used her thighs on him, a vicelike

grip on his firm prick. The outer skin shucked back and forth as he sawed in and out of her fleshy hold. Ellen kept her finger very busy in Suzie's cunt, and she could feel the simmering stew grow hotter as she stirred it.

Marlon gasped and his cock began to squirt thick white cum onto Ellen, the spunk spurting out of him like a faulty fire hose. She was drenched by the torrent as it splashed onto her cunt, spattering her bush and soft belly. She felt deliciously sluttish, moving her thighs to pull another and yet another gush out of Marlon's cock.

Ellen grabbed his prick with her free hand and squeezed on it, coating her fingers in his cum. She rubbed the sticky juice into her belly, matting her abundant pubic hair. Her thighs clenched around him and she sighed, noticing that his cock still remained super-stiff when it touched her flesh.

"I thought somebody was gonna get fucked, or something," she said. "Or was that just a lot of bullshit?"

"I'll show you from bullshit, bitch," Marlon said with a wicked grin. He yanked Ellen around and laid her out on the bed. Her finger flipped out of Suzie's cunt, who looked a little sorry at its sudden removal. Ellen lifted her knees, wiggling her body in a lewd invitation.

"Come on and fuck me, then!" she panted.

"If you think you can handle it!"

Marlon could: he climbed on board, and she eased his cock into her fuck-hole. All the watching had made her slick and wet inside, and he plunged straight into her pussy with surprising ease. His wiry pubic hair kissed her pussy-lips and the fat shaft stretched her cunt's mouth widely.

His body came down upon hers. He was a big man, the heaviest she'd ever fucked, and she felt a little crushed beneath him. In fact, a gorilla came to mind and she almost laughed out loud. Now and then she felt the breath being pressed out of her body. But the rapid, stabbing thrusts of his cock opened her pussy right up, and at its base where it was thickest, it stimulated her clitoris beautifully, which more than made up for the discomfort or any involuntary associations with big apes.

"I'm fucking you, baby!" Marlon gasped, thrusting his cock. "You see what I'm doing to her?" He looked at Suzie. "Can you see my big hard cock fucking this sweet tight cunt?"

"I see it, Mister, and it look good!" Suzie laughed throatily, sliding around to rub her slender, exciting body against his.

She reached down to caress his prick as it moved in and out of Ellen, and she got herself a few feels of pussy too.

Her nimble fingers made straight for Ellen's clit, and she tweaked it. Ellen began to shudder and tremble, aware that she would be climaxing before too much longer, slightly afraid that Marlon might fuck her crazy before she could enjoy her orgasm.

Marlon fucked her hard and deep, his big belly and crotch grinding passionately against hers while his cock stirred around and around inside her pussy. She had her feet in the air, kicking them around, and she was panting and moaning.

Suzie leaned down to kiss Ellen, and it was an exciting kiss. The lips moved down Ellen's face, onto her chest. Evidently Suzie intended to suck some tit. Ellen leaned back, lifting a tit toward the Oriental's puckered lips, and she sighed in gratification as the other woman took the nipple into her mouth.

Ellen climaxed suddenly, eruptively, without warning. Her cunt spasmed around Marlon's thrusting cock, but the big man didn't miss a stroke. He just kept pounding her with his savage prick. She folded her legs around the small of his back and fucked her heart out.

He pulled out of her cunt while she was still coming, and she hardly noticed. She frigged her pussy and her clit, shoving two or three fingers in her pussy to take up the slack left by the departure of his prick.

"Oh, fuck!" she gasped. "Oh fucking shit!"

Suzie was on hands and knees, her ass up in the air, her thighs spread. She opened her cunt and Marlon fucked in behind her, his prick sticking out and up. He angled the knob downward, to the invitation of her open pussy, and she pulled him in. He thrust, filling the Oriental whore in one. She wailed, gleeful and horny, and he started to fuck her mercilessly, his big belly slapping loudly against her tight, sassy buns.

His body hunched over hers as he filled her pussy with the meat of his cock. Ellen watched drooling, her fingers busy on her cunt, but she couldn't watch forever. This time she was quite sure that she wanted to be involved and she had no intention of being left out of the action again.

She ran her hands up and down Marlon's back, stroking his ass, reaching between his legs to tickle his balls then further up to stroke his asshole. She felt the shaft of his cock thrusting savagely into Suzie's cunt, and she felt the sticky juice that was oozing from Suzie's fuck-hole. Marlon's cock was so wet Ellen could scarcely hold onto it.

Ellen moved around to Suzie's front and lifted the Chinese girl's sweaty face. She came in, her tongue out, and she lapped the salty perspiration from Suzie's skin. The threesome was shaping up as the most exciting sexual experience of Ellen Fielding's life.

She straightened up and brought Suzie's face to her tits. The Oriental slut was only too eager to start eating them. Ellen gasped as Suzie bit down on a stiff nipple. But her tongue felt so good, tickling around and around, that Ellen didn't even mind the slight pain.

"Now me eat you," Suzie said. "I eat pussy while this dude fuck my ass off!"

Ellen sat down, her legs spread. She pulled Suzie's face down into her cunt and felt, for the very first time, another woman's mouth on her pussy. It was unlike any licking Ellen had ever gotten from a man. Suzie seemed to know instinctively where all the really hot spots were, and she lapped them thirstily, her tongue moving in and out of Ellen's pussy before it returned to its frenetic stimulation work.

"I know!" Suzie panted. "Why no you get underneath me? Then I eat you out good and you lick me while Marlon fucky-fuck me! You wanna do it like that? I bet he really get off watch us sixty-nine while he fuck my pussy with big hard cock!"

"Yeah," Marlon said, driving his cock hard and fast into Suzie. "I'd really like to see you gorgeous little whores sucking each other off!"

Ellen wasn't sure she was ready for this, but she was too deeply involved to say no. She got on her back and slid underneath Suzie until Marlon's thighs blocked her way. That left her face directly underneath the woman's cunt. She looked up and saw Marlon's cock fucking Suzie's splayed, hairless pussy-lips while his heavy balls swung to and fro in their big, hairy scrotal sack. Her mouth began to water with anticipation.

"Suck on her, bitch," Marlon whispered to her. "Suck her while I'm feeding her pussy with my cock!"

Ellen lifted her face up and her tongue began to work – awkwardly, it was true – on Suzie's perfect cunt. She tasted the honey-like juice that was dripping from the crack. She put her hands on Suzie's waist and started to lick in earnest.

Suzie, meanwhile, was head-down in Ellen's cunt, and there was nothing shy or tentative about the way she gobbled that gash. She'd obviously done this before, and she was very good at it. Her tongue kept returning to Ellen's clit, and she slurped it hungrily. The telltale pulsation down there alerted Ellen to the fact that she had not yet received her climax quota tonight. Another orgasm was definitely on its way.

Marlon's balls kept slapping against her forehead as she kept on licking Suzie's cunt, and she tilted her head back until the balls were flopping across her open mouth. She sucked on them while Marlon fucked Suzie, her tongue drifting up to the base of his prick as it moved in and out of the bald, velvet-soft slit.

She was sure she'd never have been able to lick Suzie if it hadn't been for the depilation job. She couldn't imagine shoving her face into a hairy pussy. But the more she licked Suzie, the more she felt that the hair might not make that much difference.

Marlon's prick came skidding out of Suzie's pussy on an off-stroke, and it rammed straight into Ellen's mouth. She gagged at the sudden thrust that filled her. It was the first time she'd had him in her mouth and he thrust three or four times, as if he were making up for lost opportunities.

She sucked hard, showing him that she knew her way around a stiff cock, and the taste of pussy that coated his length – the taste of Suzie's hot wet cunt – was almost as intoxicating as brandy. Ellen Fielding was beginning to feel like a total slut, and she loved it.

"Lemme fuck her again," Marlon said, yanking his cock out of Ellen's mouth.

She surrendered it gracelessly, nipping with her teeth as he slid out. She'd been getting very much into the swollen cock sliding across her tongue, and she resented losing it now. But as her mouth emptied, she could once more smell the arousal of Suzie's sex, and she moved upward, ready to eat some more tangy Oriental cunt.

She had her fingers in the game now, spreading Suzie's slit to expose the scarlet wetness within. She tongued into it, giving back in kind what Suzie was doing to her.

Marlon reclaimed his place in Suzie's cunt; Ellen followed him with her tongue. She licked his cock each time it slid out for a fresh stroke, and when he was fully buried in the raven-haired oriental, she was either slurping his balls or tonguing her bulging clit.

At first she'd been astonished that Suzie could have mistaken her for a whore, but now that she was into it, she was beginning to feel that maybe the almond-eyed hooker hadn't been too far off the mark. She'd sensed a kindred spirit all right – except that Ellen wasn't doing it for money. She was only here because her husband had betrayed her and she wanted to avenge herself in the most dramatic way possible. Or was she?

Taking a breather for a moment, allowing herself to bask in the glory of what Suzie's mouth was doing to her cunt, Ellen watched in rapt fascination the way Marlon's cock slid in and out of Suzie's delicate fuck-hole. She'd done her share of fucking, but she had never observed it from such an up-close, see-it-all, angle before.

She stared, licking her lips, at the jiggling sway of Marlon's balls, the slightly off-centre way in which he fucked his cock into Suzie, and the way Suzie's hairless crack spread open to receive him, then snuggled close around his fully-buried prick, like a mouth puckered to be kissed. She could hear the squishy noises as the long hard cock moved again and again into the receptive, wet gash.

Ellen was starting to think that maybe a woman knew more about eating pussy than any man could ever know. And she was growing convinced that she'd have to try this again – soon! She didn't know when, or how, or with whom, but those were small problems. If she wanted it badly enough, she'd find a way and a partner, and the more she got eaten, the more positive she was that she would need a woman to do it to her.

Ellen climaxed all over Suzie's mouth, and the Oriental buried her face in the wet explosion, giggling as she swallowed all of Ellen's girl-cum.

Marlon took his cock out of Suzie and slid its small, pointy tip back and forth through her cunt-slit. He teased her clit with it. He slapped her pussy with his stiff, wet prick, and he moved it up to tickle lasciviously at the little bud of her asshole, too. He made a teasing, tentative thrust, as if he meant to stick his cock up her ass.

Suzie coughed and shivered, raising her face from Ellen's pussy.

"Unh-uhhhh!" she groaned, looking back. "I tell you already, your cock too thick to take up my ass! If it thin all way down, I give you assfuck, but you got big horse cock, so no way!"

Ellen reached up, her hand on Marlon's balls. She squeezed them gently, feeling the heaviness of the load that they contained, then her hand slid up onto the cock-shaft. "Oh, what the hell, dude! You wanna stick it up somebody's asshole, why not try mine?"

Chapter 7

Ellen didn't have much time to consider it. Everyone was rolling around, and she was suddenly on her knees, in exactly the same position Suzie had been in a few minutes ago. Suzie was lying beneath her, sliding her tongue through Ellen's hot dripping labia, then sucking each pendulous cuntlip in turn, while Marlon was behind her, poking her asscheeks with the stiff rod of his cock.

"You got a great ass," Marlon said, his hands stroking over the magnificent spread of Ellen's buttocks and her upper thighs. "And I bet it fucks tight as a goddamn drum. Right, baby? You got yourself one tight little ass?

But it won't be nearly as tight when I'm done with it!"

Ellen shuddered.

He worked the edge of his hand up and down the crack of her ass, pressing in hard. She felt his knuckles against her anus, and she gulped.

"Me get her ready!" Suzie panted, thrusting her face up into Ellen's crotch. She snapped at the pussy-lips, humming as she nibbled them. She thrust her tongue straight into Ellen's open cunt, spearing it deep and wiggling it like an eel inside the aprehensive woman.

Removing her tongue, she spread Ellen's ass, baring her perfect little nut-brown anus. She kissed it, smacking her lips, and then licked it until Ellen began to gasp with pleasure. Suzie pulled the fleshy mounds even wider, stretching the shit-hole far enough for it to show a bit of red interior and to facilitate penetration with the tip of her tongue.

"Aahhhhh!" husked Suzie, poking with her stiff, extended tongue. She held on to Ellen's soft, rounded buttocks so tightly that Ellen was worried that the marks would be visible for days.

Ellen whined and strained, fighting back a little but not really fighting. Each time she lurched forward, dragging her ass away from Suzie's tongue, she ended the motion by thrusting it right back, straight into Suzie's

hungry face.

She felt very dirty, having her shitter tongue-washed by this horny Oriental slut, but she also felt very, very good, and she was beginning to drool at the thought of having Marlon's stiff cock rammed up that same tight hole.

"Oh, yeah, eat my shit, you cunt!" Ellen moaned, squeezing her tits while she fed her asshole to Suzie.

Then the licking was interrupted, and she felt the long thick weight of Marlon's prick sliding through her crotch. It parted her meaty pussy-lips, stroked the wet slickness of her pussy-slit, the tip scraping back and forth over the hot bud of her aroused clit. Marlon slid his cock back and forth, coating it in her ooze of fuck-juices.

He pushed his cock-knob into her pussy, soaking it in Ellen's slippery wetness. She moaned, feeling him inside her again.

"Oh, fuck me!" she cried. "Fuck me deep and hard!"

But he was only paying her pussy a short visit, just getting his cock lubed for the real job.

"I'll give it to you deep and hard in a minute, bitch!" he growled. "But first I have to get good and wet so I don't rip your shitter open."

The coarse voice tone, the ugly, nasty

words – they thrilled her unbelievably. He was going to use her like a piece of meat, and she could not have been happier if he'd eaten her shit.

"Now do it! Fuck me!" she moaned. "Fuck me in the ass!"

Suzie was playing with Ellen's pussy and asshole, using her fingers to make Ellen even more excited, if that was even possible. She pulled Ellen's anal sphincter wide open by inserting two hook-like fingers and prying the tight muscle wide open. Ellen thought she could feel the air rush in to her open rectum. Never had she felt quite so vulnerable with two pairs of eyes inspecting her most secret orifice as it was forced to gape redly open.

Ellen bit her lip as the sexy black-haired woman alternated this wild action by corkscrewing the tips of her fingers into her rectal cavity, twisting them around and around as if she meant to drill her way straight into her guts. Ellen screamed. She was still so goddamn new to this sort of love-play, and the sudden penetration of Suzie's fingers made her shudder with a sort of horrified thrill. As Suzie began to work them in and out, Ellen's skin continued to crawl, but it was a nice kind of creepiness.

Her asshole was tight but willing. It fitted snugly around Suzie's fingers, milking at the length of the digits while they pushed in and out. Ellen gasped and shivered, her ass lifting and falling. She held onto her own breasts very tightly, the nipples rigid and long between her squeezing fingers. Soon they were as hard as twin bullets.

"I think she good and ready, stud!" Suzie grinned at Marlon, easing her fingers out of Ellen. The muscles clenched at it, reluctant to let go. "Now you fuck her! Fuck asshole with big, long, sweet cock of yours, baby! Me want to see you stick it in her good!"

She stretched out again, teasing Ellen's cunt with long, delicate fingers. From time to time she would lick upward, tickling the clit or molesting the dripping wet lips of her cunt. But the main action was going to take place a little further back, and Ellen trembled with increased trepidation, as she waited fearfully for Marlon to fill her rectum with his big, stiff prick.

He was behind her, on his knees, and she could feel the heat of his body even though he wasn't touching her, except now and then when his stiff cock bumped against the trembling cheeks of her ass. Suzie's tongue was all over her cunt, her clit, and she was about to crawl out of her tingling skin.

"Oh, goddamn you," she said, her voice suddenly small and quavering. "Will you please get on and fuck me? I can't stand the suspense!"

He took her at her word. The head of his cock suddenly poised itself against her shiny-slick brown star, and he shoved, testing the waters. She wasn't as tight as she might have been, since Suzie's stretch-and-ream-operations of the past few minutes. The small, pointy tip of his cock entered her anal ring with almost ridiculous ease, nosing its way past the tight, incredibly sensitive half-inch of muscle that was Ellen's quivering asshole.

And then he shoved a bit harder and the thicker portion of his cock pushed itself through her snug ass-ring.

"Aaaahhhhh!" Ellen shrieked. This wasn't just uncomfortable: this was definitely painful. This was bigger than anything she had ever experienced in her entire life entering her bowels. It was like succeeding in taking the most agonizing, constipated shit, only in reverse.

She'd had him in her pussy, but it wasn't quite the same thing. Her cunt was snug, but elastic – far more so than her asshole, and she could feel every pulsation in Marlon's cock as he continued to slowly fuck his cock in. He wasn't trying to bust her ass, but he was determined to accept the assfuck she had so bravely offered him.

Suzie's wet tongue made the initial pain a lot easier to bear.

Suzie kept on licking. Ellen couldn't believe

how wild it felt to have another woman's tongue on her pussy – inside her pussy – licking her inside out. It was so different to the way men went down on her, and as she enjoyed the frisky slurps and licks and kisses, she could feel an orgasm building in every part of her genital area. The pain grew even less. Now it was merely as if someone had stuffed a baseball bat up her ass...

"Uhhhh!" Marlon grunted, thrusting the full length of his cock into Ellen's shitter. She rocked and rolled her ass against him, absorbing the feel of his cock, the incredibly stuffed sensation of being so utterly full of him. Her asshole was so tight she didn't know how he expected to fuck her. Just getting the thing in her was miracle enough.

He pulled back, and it felt like he was yanking her guts out along with his retreating cock. He pulled maybe half his cock out of Ellen, and then he shoved it straight into her. It felt like a concrete turd had changed its mind halfway out her ass and was crawling back up her shit-chute. She loved every inch of it.

"Oh, fucking shit, it hurts!" she gasped. "But... don't fuckin' stop it!"

He didn't stop. Neither did Suzie. She seemed to have a definite pussy fixation, eating her way thirstily into Ellen's cunt, using her fingers to tease the outer labia and occasionally slide into her vagina while she nibbled and sucked the clit and inner cuntlips. Ellen heard Marlon grunt with enjoyment, and somehow she knew Suzie was also tonguing his cock as it fucked in and out of her ass. She hoped, for Suzie's sake, that it wasn't too dirty.

Ellen looked down. She was staring into Suzie's crotch. The Chinese girl's legs were open wide, and the wet slick pink of her cunt was showing, the lips parted as if they wanted to be kissed, little beads of moisture oozing slowly from within the lovely prostitute's body.

Ellen lowered her face and started to lick Suzie's belly, her tongue edging downward to the cunt itself. The increasingly familiar smell of pussy filled her nostrils, and saliva filled her mouth. She slobbered her drool onto Suzie's smooth, hairless crotch and began to massage it into the flesh with her lapping tongue.

Marlon kept fucking her ass with his cock. It hurt. He was still having a hard time moving in and out, but he fucked her in short strokes that jolted and jarred her entire body and made her ass spasm in response.

She was sobbing with pleasure-pain now. As he continued to sodomise her briskly, it still hurt, but now it was a different sort of pain. Each stroke was a new kind of agonizing bliss. Ellen had been raised in gentility, with all the pampering money could buy. This was the first time her precious body had ever known such rough treatment. The cock reamed her tight ass, fucking mercilessly as Marlon got into the thrill of screwing this lovely woman in her bottom hole, knowing there was not a goddamn thing she could do except take it.

Ellen Fielding was learning things about herself that she had never before guessed. The degradation and pain of being fucked up the ass were turning her on like crazy. This man thought she was some slut, some whore, and he was fucking her like a whore – fucking her where she shit. His cock cared only about its own pleasure, the sweet hot tightness of being crammed up her asshole. And she was wiggling and writhing and urging him with the gyrations of her body to keep on fucking her just that way.

Even more wild, she was nose-deep in Suzie's pussy, lapping the slippery crack and sliding her tongue into it for a more lingering taste of the Oriental's cunt-cream, and her tongue tingled and burned with a growing urgency, a blistering frenzy of arousal.

Conversely, her own cunt was full of Suzie's tongue, and she knew that she was coating it with a big helping of her fuck-juices. Ellen's clit twitched and vibrated under the attack of Suzie's fingers, and she licked at Suzie's engorged pink pleasure bean too, feeling within herself each spurt of pleasure that her tongue gave to Suzie.

Marlon kept his cock busy, but Ellen's asshole was enlarging now, accommodating itself to the fatness that filled her. He could get almost a full stroke, and he was taking advantage of it. His cock emerged from her shitter, only the knob still wedged within her tight ass-ring, and he plunged home with a driving down stroke that made Ellen scream into Suzie's pussy. But it was a scream of pleasure, and the tears that still flowed down her cheeks were becoming tears of joy.

"Oh, fuck me!" she moaned, her head shaking so frenetically she could hardly find the time to lick Suzie's cunt. "Fuck my ass with your big hard cock!"

She was only sorry now that she had always rejected Meredith when he'd suggested this act. She wished she'd tried it long ago.

She spread Suzie's cunt wide, exposing the coral pink of the interior, eating it with her eyes as well as her tongue. There was something truly beautiful and mysterious about the texture of the pussy that filled her gaze, a fleshy flower, a lovely orchid.

The slickness of the flesh tempted her tongue. She fucked through with her tongue, pushing it deep into Suzie, relishing the far stronger taste of cunt that she found so much further within. She drew her tongue out and let her saliva dribble onto Suzie's hard clit, feeling it throb beneath the caresses of her tongue.

Her anal tightness yielded dramatically as Marlon's prick fucked in and out of Ellen. She was still a snug fit around the swollen barrel of his cock, but he penetrated her again and again with virtually no problem, except when he went too deep and the glans of his pointy penis banged into her guts as if he wanted to spill his load as far up her rectal cavity as possible.

He worked her legs as he fucked her, sliding her slick thighs around his body and squeezing them around himself. It made her ass clench even more tightly on his cock, and the enhanced sensations made Ellen whimper and shriek.

She felt the unmistakable tremors of orgasm shooting through Suzie's pussy. Ellen began to lick faster. She was aware of the action in her ass, but it took a back seat for now to the struggle to get Suzie off. She tongued the woman's pussy, poking in and out, worshipping the other woman's clit.

Suzie bounced and shook and moaned. Her body was so frantic that she drove Ellen upward again and again, each convulsion making Ellen bang more hotly into the cock that plugged her ass. Suzie wasn't doing much cunt-eating right now, but that was okay. Marlon's cock was providing all the stimulation Ellen could handle.

She drank the juices that oozed from Suzie's fuck-hole, and she tongued into her cunt, hungry for more.

Beneath her, Suzie was moaning and giggling.

"Oh, I come now!" she squealed. "Make me squirt, baby! Lick that cunt! Eat Suzie's clit! Mmm, get me off!"

Marlon yanked his cock out of Ellen's asshole and shoved it straight into Suzie's mouth. She sucked at it, gagging as it went too deep, but she didn't stop sucking, and Marlon gave her three or four heartfelt thrusts before he freed his cock from her lips and slam-dunked it up Ellen's shitter once more.

The sensation of having him inside her again was all that Ellen needed. Her head jerked upward and she said, "Oh, you motherfucker! You're making me come tooooooooo!"

Chapter 8

Marlon kept fucking Ellen, and she screamed with each thrust. Suzie had a finger or two up her pussy, and Ellen squirmed back and forth, alternately impaling herself on the cock and the digits. She was holding a tit with one hand, Suzie's cunt with the other, and she shuddered as her asshole refilled, time after time, with the horny stabs of Marlon's prick.

"I'm gonna come!" Marlon panted from behind her.

Ellen was in the throes of a big orgasm, but she couldn't miss his words, and she jerked forward desperately, disengaging her ass from his prick. Turning around, she saw him already shoving his prick into Suzie's mouth.

"Don't be a hog, cunt!" she gasped, throwing herself down upon the sweat-soaked Oriental.

Her tits lay full and firm upon Suzie's, and her pussy was shoved into the black-haired girl's crotch, her dark hair gritty and ticklish on Suzie's smooth cunt. She forced the Oriental whore to release Marlon's prick, and she sucked it into her own lips, pursing them around the thick throbbing shaft as she took it in.

She sucked wildly, crazily, gnawing and pressuring his cock. Suzie was moaning and scratching and whining, and Ellen allowed the Oriental another suck or two before she took it back into her own mouth.

Her mouth watered as she watched Suzie sucking, and then it would be her turn, and she took him in greedily, until the unspoken plea in Suzie's brown eyes inspired her to share. Not for one moment did it worry her that this hard tube of flesh had been in such a nasty place.

Her body still tingled from her orgasm, and the constant rubbing of her pussy against Suzie's kept her fires blazing high. She wolfed the cock, surrendering it with reluctance, waiting for the moment it would enter her mouth once more.

Marlon's balls hung in Suzie's eyes. It wasn't a great angle for Suzie to suck from, but it was a perfect shot for Marlon's tool into Ellen's mouth, and she took advantage of it.

Her tongue caressed him whorishly, licking the hot hard shaft of cock as he thrust in and out, and if he had any complaints about the value he was getting for his money, he didn't mention them.

But he'd had a hell of a workout, and she knew he couldn't last much longer. He had his eyes shut, and his prick was trembling spasmodically as it worked in and out of their mouths. Ellen tasted the jizz already oozing from his knob, and she sucked more desperately, anxious for him to empty his balls down her throat.

"Give me some!" Suzie gasped, grabbing for his cock.

Ellen moaned in disgust as she had to release it, and she watched Suzie suck the knob into her mouth, closing her lips tightly around it.

She made a kissy-face at Ellen, gurgling as she sucked the end of Marlon's prick. Her tongue was working feverishly, to judge from the way her cheeks jiggled. She rolled her eyes in delight and she kept on sucking.

Ellen stroked his cock-shaft up and down while Suzie nursed his prick-knob. Suzie made gulping sounds of pleasure and gluttony, and then her mouth opened wide and the cock came bouncing out, slapping Ellen in the face. As it touched her nose, it started to squirt.

"Yes!" Marlon shouted. "Oh, eat my cum, you fucking whores!"

He came a gusher, the jizz boiling out of his balls. It splattered both women's faces. Ellen was still holding him, and she sucked the shaft, milking out his load. The women were kissing, licking one another, and drinking the gooey cum that puddled on their skin.

Ellen got the end of his prick between her lips and took his last squirt square on the tongue, savouring the pearly slime as it oozed down her throat. Then she bent down and resumed lapping the spilled-out jizz from Suzie's face.

Marlon collapsed, breathing heavily.

"That was the best, girls. That was the best ever."

He got up with difficulty and staggered off to the bathroom where they could hear the shower going for a long time.

Suzie took a roll of bills from her purse. She peeled off five hundreds and handed them to Ellen, who stared at the money, not quite believing that it was actually being offered to her.

"You were great," Suzie said. "Really great."

Ellen looked up sharply. Suzie sounded different. More sophisticated.

She took the bills, uncertain what to do with them.

"I mean it," Suzie said. "I think that was the best ever. You were worth five hundred, and more. Listen, is there a number where we can get in touch with you? Marlon and I are in town three or four times a year. We'd love to see you again."

Ellen stared.

Suzie laughed.

"Oh, you still don't get it?" she asked, taking Ellen's hand. "Marlon's my husband. We like to play games. One of our favorites is two whores on a john. I mean, please don't be offended! I like you. In fact I like you very much. And I would come up with another hundred if you'd let me show you just how much..."

Marlon reappeared, already dressed. "I'll be back in a little while," he said. "After that workout, I think I need a drink."

And he left them alone together.

* * *

Ellen Fielding was truly shocked now. Suzie was rolling her all over the bed, sliding her mouth up and down Ellen's body. She covered Ellen's mouth in a tongue-scorching kiss, while her body insinuated itself between Ellen's thighs, and she rubbed her cunt insistently against Ellen's crotch, sighing as her hairless pussy stroked Ellen's own, hirsute cunt.

She pressed her smaller, springy tits with their still-hard nipples, onto Ellen's chest, her hands full of Ellen's tits. She dug her fingers into the spongy tit-flesh, squeezing until Ellen's big nipples stiffened, duelling deliciously with her own sensitive little buds. Her drool flowed into Ellen's mouth, and her tongue was as fuck-crazed as a stiff cock, poking in and out. She thrust it deep and she made it wiggle like a snake.

"Marlon loves to fuck two women at once," Suzie whispered, bubbles of spit frothing on her lips and sticking to Ellen's mouth. "I like a little one-on-one. He left so we could have a bit of privacy. Let's make the most of it, darling!"

She moved downward, making for the points of tit that her eager fingers had teased to erection. Looking up, excitement gleaming in her eyes, she licked the nipples until they glistened, then sucked them into her mouth. She squeezed the tits together so that her mouth didn't have to travel so far, and she worked her head back and forth, biting one tit and then the other.

Ellen lay back, opening her legs a little wider so Suzie could ease her body even closer. The friction of their cunts was creating a vibrant, exciting heat in Ellen's crotch. She slid her hands up and down Suzie's back while the bare-cunted Oriental fed on her tits.

"Yes, yes, keep on licking me!"

Suzie had no intention of stopping! She bit and chewed at the hard nipples, eating them until Ellen gasped and moaned. Ellen rocked back. Her legs curled around Suzie's and she used her thigh muscles to pull her new lover in closer still, increasing the hot contact of their aroused pussies.

She pulled Suzie's face up and kissed the drool off the Oriental's wet lips. This time it was Ellen's turn to get aggressive. She put her hands on Suzie's cheeks and forced her lips open. Suzie giggled and played reluctant.

Ellen pressed with her tongue until the Oriental's mouth opened and Ellen's tongue thrust inside. Then Ellen rolled Suzie over and mounted her hot body.

She was all over Suzie. She moved down to the tits, licking them until they were so wet her tongue couldn't keep from skidding on the small but firm apple-like breasts. Her hand was down between Suzie's thighs. Suzie gasped and bucked.

She wiggled her finger in and out of the woman's wet cunt, wiggling it deep inside just for the pleasure of watching Suzie squirm. She'd already tasted her pussy, but she was hungry to taste it again. She left off sucking tit and kissed her way down Suzie's belly, toward the spot where her cunt-hair used to be. It was impossible to miss that location.

She pushed again, as if she meant to stuff her entire fist up Suzie's fuck-hole. The Oriental squealed and writhed and spread her legs wider, opening her cunt to the attack. Ellen's face was down between Suzie thighs now. She bit and chewed the insides of them, leaving teeth-marks in the Oriental's creamy flesh.

Suzie's hands combed through Ellen's hair.

"Oh, yes, eat my pussy!" she moaned. "You do it soooo good, baby!"

Ellen took her finger out and offered it to Suzie. The giggling Oriental sucked it into her mouth as eagerly and earnestly as she'd sucked it up her cunt. She seemed to like the taste of her juices. She wasn't the only one.

Ellen pushed her nose into Suzie's crotch, sniffing. The pussy muscles sucked at her nose. All she could breathe was the flavor of the Oriental's arousal.

Suzie lifted her knees and her cunt seemed to gape open. Ellen replaced her nose with her tongue, poking it up the hole until she could advance no farther. She licked the hole inside-out, smacking her lips in pleasure. She grew more and more positive that she was going to be eating a lot more pussy in the future, though she had no idea right now where she was going to find any more pussy to eat.

The more she licked, the wetter Suzie got. She was starting to get the distinct impression that the petite Oriental was a lot more interested in women than men.

Her hands were under Suzie's ass, pulling the Oriental's pussy up into her face. She had a firm, supple ass. It was a tactile pleasure just to have her fingers on it. As she sucked pussy, she alternately spread and compressed the woman's asscheeks. Suzie's heels were braced on the mattress, and she had her ass completely off the bed. Ellen was up on her knees now, angling into the ecstatic cunt.

She moved her tongue downward, onto the tiny opening of the Oriental's asshole. It was so snug and delicate Ellen couldn't help wondering how in the fuck Suzie ever managed to squeeze a turd out the hole. Even when she licked it and diddled the tight ring with her tongue, it remained tight, sealed, almost reluctant to get involved.

Suzie was whining and moaning. Not much doubt she enjoyed having her ass licked. Ellen smiled, a nasty idea coming to her. She let Suzie drop down onto the bed and then she rolled the quivering Oriental onto her belly. She opened her thighs again and crawled between them, face pushing onto Suzie's pussy from the rear.

The Oriental moved up on her knees, her ass lifting, and Ellen followed its rise with her tongue. She was licking Suzie's pussy from back to front, her tongue sliding onto the hot pink clit from underneath. But she kept bringing her tongue back to the asshole, ravishing it again and again.

She could feel the little hole getting more relaxed. She poked with her tongue, and the ring yielded a bit, allowing her momentary shallow penetration.

"Oh, you're so dirty!" Suzie giggled. "I like that in a girl!"

Ellen bent slightly and brought her tits into play. She caressed the Oriental's pussy with them. She even spread the cunt-lips and guided the peak of a nipple into the woman's pussy. She thought it might make Suzie feel good, and she was inclined to think it might make her feel good too. She was right on both counts. The woman's pussy mouth sucked at her nipple.

She tried her nipple on Suzie's asshole, too. Much tighter, but just as much fun to tit-fuck. Slobber ran from her mouth and down her chin, spilling onto the curves of her tits.

Glancing about, she saw – still lying on the rumpled bed – the vibrator she'd used on herself in the encounter with Marlon. The batteries had been almost drained, but she thought there might be a little life still in them. She grabbed the thing and flipped it on. The buzzing was weak, but it was enough for what Ellen had in mind.

"Let's play with this toy," she said, buzzing Suzie's pussy with the vibrator. "Bet you've had it down there a few times, right, baby?"

"Mmmmm, right!" Suzie moaned. "Slide it in and out of me – not too deep – just in and out! And tickle my clit, too! I really like that!"

She worked the tip into Suzie's cunt-hole, easing it gently in and out, just as she had requested. The Oriental began to throb and whimper, obviously getting deeper and deeper into her sexual possession.

Ellen took the initiative, shoving the vibrator a little further into her new friend's cunt.

"Ohhhhhhhhh!" Suzie moaned. "Not so deep!"

But she took it, and Ellen smirked in satisfaction. She took a tighter grip on the base of the dildo and pushed it until her

fingertips were flush against Suzie's ass-crack. The Oriental moaned again. Ellen rotated the vibrator inside her.

"Fuck me, oh, fuck me, baby!" Suzie groaned, her voice as hypnotic as the muted buzz of the vibrator.

Ellen fucked her.

There was an incredible sense of power, of control, in the act of working the dildo in and out. She was beginning to understand, for the first time, how a man must feel shoving his cock up a woman's cunt. As she used the dildo, she was busy with her tongue on Suzie's asshole, continuing the arousal she'd already begun there.

Ellen kept the dildo busy, and she kept her tongue busy, too. Suzie's asshole didn't taste particularly shitty. Ellen probably wouldn't have stopped even if it had. Her tongue was prodding the little hole, and the little hole was expanding a bit more each time it got licked.

Now it was time to use her finger.

She straightened up, keeping the vibrator moving, and she began to push at Suzie's ass-ring with her middle finger. Suzie squealed at the feel of a finger attacking her ass, but she didn't ask Ellen to stop, and Ellen wouldn't have stopped even if she'd been asked.

The finger entered Suzie's shitter. The muscles gripped her finger in a wet, sticky – almost greasy – heat. Ellen prodded a time or two, and then it seemed that the Oriental's asshole took over the work. Ellen could feel her finger being drawn in and out.

"Oooohhhhh!" Suzie gasped. "You're gonna make me come if you don't stop that! And if you stop, I'll rip your tits off!"

Ellen smiled. She felt very smug and self-satisfied right now. But she had one more ace up her sleeve. With a wrench of her wrist, she yanked the dildo out of Suzie's cunt, then lay down on her back, beneath the Oriental's uplifted crotch. Her finger came out of Suzie's asshole, and she moved the dildo up to the finger-dilated hole while her tongue began to move up and down the slick wet crack of Suzie's pussy.

"Oh, you dirty bitch!" Suzie cried. "You're not gonna... nooooo!"

Ellen put the tip of the vibrator square against the Oriental's shitter and gave it a stabbing thrust. Her finger had reamed the tight ass to some extent. It was still as tight as hell, but the opening wasn't nearly as snug as it had been, and the end of the vibrator entered Suzie.

The vibrator pushed its way up Suzie's shit-hole while Ellen feasted on the Oriental's sloppy cunt. Ellen was squeezing her own thighs together, massaging the bun of her own pussy, and she could feel heat building dramatically inside it. Suzie wasn't the only one with a wet cunt.

She kept on tonguing the woman's clit and the cunt while she moved the dildo in short thrusts up Suzie's asshole.

If she'd kept at it long enough, she could probably have shoved the thing so far up Suzie that it came out her mouth. But Suzie climaxed long before that point, and, to her own surprise, Ellen's orgasm came only a moment or two later. The power and the sex, and the scent of raw pussy sent her hurtling over the edge, though, and the two women collapsed into a sweat-soaked heap of flesh.

Suzie pulled Ellen up, kissing her thirstily.

"God, that was fantastic," she said. "Here's our number and you've gotta give us yours! Even if Marlon can't make it, I'm gonna come back for some more of that sweet hot cunt of yours, baby! Oh, you've earned your money tonight!"

"I just try to keep the customer satisfied," Ellen said, and grinned.

Chapter 9

With the money – six hundred dollars – tucked into her stocking top, Ellen Fielding felt like a satisfied whore. She was ready for bed – and a long sleep.

Back at the apartment, there was a message from Meredith. He had decided to stay a couple more days in Los Angeles and suggested that she return to Seattle. Disconsolately, Ellen fixed herself a sandwich and salad and sat down to look at the tube with a big glass of white wine. After she had finished eating, she took a quick shower, brushed her teeth, got into bed and switched out the light. She was almost asleep before her head hit the pillow.

* * *

The next day, Ellen drove around a bit, with no real destination in mind. She wasn't ready to go to the Cabin just yet. And she was still trying to decide what to do about her husband and his treachery.

Maybe it was partly her fault. Maybe she'd been a little conservative in bed. Maybe that's why he'd taken on another woman. From what she'd seen through the window that day at the Cabin, it was fairly obvious that Nancy McGuinness was not at all old-fashioned when it came to sex.

The little redheaded slut had giggled so gleefully at the prospect of taking Meredith's cock in her pussy, her mouth, and her asshole.

The bitch had even wrapped her super-sized tits around his cock as if to let him squirt off in her freckled face.

But then Ellen didn't feel very conservative now, either, considering what she got up to just recently. She found herself thinking about the bush of red hair around Nancy's cunt. Meredith appeared to enjoy nuzzling his face in it. Ellen wondered if she might not find it just as tasty.

It was already getting dark. She passed a telephone booth and, on an impulse, stopped the car. Although she knew what the result would be, she needed to be sure. She dialled Meredith's hotel in Los Angeles and waited for the switchboard to ring his room. A woman answered. She had a soft voice and identified herself as Mrs. Fielding. Ellen apologized for getting the wrong number and hung up.

She got back into the car, shaking with anger. She was in no fit state to drive now and looked around for a place to stop. She was near a lumber mill belonging to Roeberd Inc. and could see that there was a light on in the little hut at the gate where the night watchman usually sat. Ellen parked the car and walked up to the small wooden building. Standing on tiptoe, she peeked inside.

She saw three guys sitting at a table, playing cards, sipping whisky, and shooting the shit. The men didn't notice her, which gave Ellen a moment to look them over.

Two of them were young, probably fresh out of high school – one a greaser type with slick hair, the other a sandy-blond, both wearing jeans and sleeveless T-shirts that showed off their well-developed biceps. The third man was older, perhaps in his late thirties. His face was turned away, but there was something familiar about the back of his head.

"You better have a royal flush," said the younger of the two studs, taking a bill off the stack of dollars in front of him. He put it down in the centre of the table and then poured himself a drink. "If you don't, I'm going home a rich man tonight."

The other stud filled his own paper cup. He was out of the hand.

"I'm going home a horny man," he said. "Mary Lou's on the rag. There's no fuckin' justice."

Ellen cleared her throat.

"Hey," she said, leaning against the doorpost, "who do I have to fuck to get a drink around here?"

They all turned, and Ellen's jaw dropped when she saw the face of the third man. It was big Jim Murray, the Roeberds area manager.

"Shouldn't that be 'whom'?" commented the large man, dryly.

Jim's expression didn't change as he stared back at Ellen, though it was obvious he recognized her. He laid his cards down and he looked at her calmly. She could see that he wasn't going to let the others know her real identity or give them any clue of what they had been up to together. In other words, he was acting as if he had never met her in his life and letting her call the shots here.

The guy who wasn't going to fuck Mary Lou stood up.

"You could always start with me," he said, picking up the bottle and holding it out.

"Good a place as any," Ellen said, moving toward the table.

Jim Murray leaned back in his chair. He had a cigarette in one hand, a paper cup in the other. He tilted his head to one side and watched Ellen through narrowed eyes. But by that time, the dark young greaser with the athletic build was standing in front of her, and she reached for the bottle he held in his hand.

"Cheers," she said, tipping it and pouring a shot down her throat. The cheap whisky burned all the way down, where it lit a small fire, somewhere deep in her belly.

No one was playing cards now. The other young guy was on his feet, his thumbs hitched in the belt loops of his jeans. His T-shirt was skin-tight, and he had the most gorgeous body Ellen had ever seen in her life.

Ellen's eyes drifted downward, checking out the front of his tight jeans. The bulge of his cock was plain to see. The corners of Ellen's mouth lifted in a smile. She took another swig from the bottle and said, "Well, I suppose you want to be paid for the whisky, right, mister?"

She put the bottle down on the card table and went to the man who had handed it to her. She pushed herself against him, first with the tits, then coming in at crotch level. He was about Ellen's size, maybe a tad taller, and she stared into his eyes from an inch away while she stroked his body with her own. Her mouth was open, the tip of her tongue showing between the lips. She slid her tongue along her lips, moistening them, and her eyes sparkled a challenge.

"Man, I don't fuckin' believe this!" he gasped, grabbing her ass and squeezing her body tight against his.

Her legs spread, and she surrounded him with them. She thrust her cunt vigorously, massaging his crotch until she felt the spirit beginning to flow life into his cock. It hardened inside his pants as she kept her body in action.

He fondled her ass excitedly, grinding her ass in his hands. She pushed herself into him, moving her crotch up and down against his cock and balls. She could feel the length of his prick in there. Her tongue fucked into his mouth and her drool merged with his.

Her hands encircled him, and she cupped

his ass. She stroked up and down, feeling the ripples of his muscles. She pushed her hands down inside the top of his pants, inside his shorts, hungry to feel bare flesh under her fingers.

She opened her mouth for a kiss. His breath tasted of whisky. So did hers. She was starting to feel the booze at the back of her head, a tingling buzz. She could feel her teddy crotch getting damp, and there was a throbbing at the point of her hardening clit.

He turned her around, backing Ellen up against the edge of the table. She parked her ass on the side, and he lifted her skirt. His hand moved on the insides of her thighs, back and forth, his fingertips brushing across the crotch of her flimsy, one-piece undergarment. Suddenly he thrust his hand inside the leg opening and got himself a fistful of her wet cunt.

His finger entered her pussy after scraping the hard bud of her clit, and she spread her legs, the muscles automatically drawing him deeper into her fuck-hole. She squeezed with her cunt, milking his finger, coating it in the wetness that was already flowing like piss from her pussy.

"Oh, shit," he said. "This bitch is primed and ready!"

He brought his hand out and waved the fingers in front of his buddy's face. The other guy sniffed and grinned. Jim Murray still sat on the other side of the table, sipping at his paper cup of whisky.

They were both on her then, getting her out of her dress and sliding down the straps of her teddy to bare her jiggling tits. Each of them took a tit in hand, pinching the nipples to make them stand up even bigger and stiffer. One of them leaned down to take a wet-mouthed suck. Ellen stroked his head while he fed at her tit, and she gurgled in satisfaction.

The other guy was pulling the teddy downward, then off her feet. Now she was naked except for her shoes and stockings.

"What are your names?" she asked throatily. "Introductions are normally considered civilized."

"I'm Bob," said the one who had struck her as the hunkier of the two. He was rubbing his hand across her belly, just above the upper edge of her pussy-bush. The bulge in his tight jeans had become enormous.

"And I'm Randy," the darker one said, licking drool off his lips as he raised his face from Ellen's wet, slobber-coated tits.

"The old fart over there is Jim Murray," Bob said. "I think he's too old to get excited. Holy shit, Randy, will ya feel this?" He slid his hands appreciatively over her smooth, creamy asscheeks. "She's no cheap whore, and that's for sure – she's pure class!"

"Shut up and take out your cock," she said. "You're getting for free what the last guy paid six hundred dollars for."

She slid down off the edge of the table.

She dropped to her knees, the two young guys facing her from either side, and she waited for them to unzip. They got the message, hauling their semi-rigid cocks out. Ellen smiled, took one in each hand, and began to stroke them with a sensual rhythm.

They weren't entirely hard yet, and that was good. She enjoyed the feel of a prick getting stiff in her hand, or inside her mouth. She caressed them a few more times, then leaned toward Bob and stroked her tongue across the end of his prick.

It throbbed on her tongue. She pulled it into her mouth, sucking like a guppy in little thirsty swallows that moved the knob of his cock in and out. It stiffened quickly, until the fatness of his helmet-shaped glans almost gagged her. She sucked it across her tongue, making it wet, and making him horny.

"Another one over here, baby," Randy said, and she turned quickly, releasing Bob's cock and sliding her moist lips down over the tip of Randy's.

They were pretty well hung young guys, and their cocks pulsated with the freshness and vitality of youth. They tasted and smelled delicious to her, clean male sweat mixed with a certain musky odour that drove her wild. Her mouth slid lower and lower down the rising shaft of Randy's cock. It expanded between her lips, across her tongue, beginning to simmer with the heat of lust.

She was playing with Bob's prick while she ate Randy's, but she ached for another taste of him. Ellen turned again, and opened her mouth to Bob's prick, purring as it slid home. Her fist moved erotically on Randy's cock, making sure he stayed good and hard.

She got a glimpse of Jim Murray. He was watching them, quiet, apparently unconcerned by what was going on. For a second she felt self-conscious, embarrassed and even a little annoyed, like she was putting on a show for his benefit, but it soon passed. She didn't really have time to worry about it. She was eating two hot hard cocks, one after the other, her head bobbing back and forth from one prick to the next. They glistened with her bubble-flecked saliva, and their taste coated her tongue.

She squirmed a bit where she knelt, bringing her thighs together so they could squeeze against the excited bun of her pussy, and she felt wetness down there that compared to the drool she had spilled on Bob's and Randy's cocks. As she sucked, she rocked herself up and down, accentuating the pressure on her pussy.

"Shit, what a mouth!" one of them sighed, fucking deep into Ellen.

She gagged at the thrust of his cock, but she forced her throat to relax, and suddenly she was gulping him straight to the balls. She made gasping, throaty noises around his prick as it began to fuck in and out quickly. Ellen gagged again, hardly able to keep up with him but too horny now to make him stop and feeling triumphant she had deep-throated a man for the first time in her life.

It was Randy. He had a long, fairly thin cock, but it felt gigantic as it fucked down her throat. She eased her face out of the way and let her tongue slide up and down on his prick as it swished back and forth before her mouth.

"Get your fucking pants off, I wanna suck your balls, too!" she gasped, taking Bob's cock in both hands and lapping like a hungry dog at the globular tip.

He wasn't circumcised, and she played with the foreskin as she licked him.

"Now you get naked too," she said, releasing his cock and turning her attention to Randy, who was stripped to his socks and T-shirt. He had a really slim waist, and a skinny ass, and his prick stuck out like a pipe. His balls were huge, and Ellen went straight for them.

She leaned down, turning her face upward.

He opened his legs, standing straddled, his hands braced on her head. She nibbled his balls, pulling the hair with her teeth. Her fist was full of his prick, and she masturbated him energetically while her tongue slid around the base of his balls, up into the crack of his ass, then down again.

She licked his hard cock, moving up and down the shaft. Coming to the cock-knob, she kissed it wetly, then slapped it with her tongue. Dribbles of clear precum were already oozing from his piss-slit. She scooped them up with her fingers, smeared them down the shaft, and licked them away.

Her lips fitted over the helmet-like knob of his prick, and she sucked it juicily, purring while she slid it in and out in short swallows.

She used her tongue furiously, sliding it around the edges of his cock-knob. Her hand clutched his balls.

"Aw, please don't do that, baby," he whined, "you're gonna blow my balls off!"

Still on her knees, she turned quickly. Bob was out of his jeans and shorts now, and his erect cock bobbed toward her, but she evaded it with a giggle. She wasn't finished with Randy yet. She grabbed one of the paper cups from the table. It contained perhaps half an inch of whisky. She swirled it, her hand still busy on Randy's prick, and she moved toward him with the cup.

"Squirt in here," she said. "I want to see the jizz flying from your prick!"

She angled his cock downward and held the cup just beneath his cock. Leaning down, she licked his cock kittenishly, stroking up the shaft.

"Cum, baby!" she whispered, her lips fluttering against his cock-head. "Cum for me!"

"Ah!" he sighed, and his cock quivered in her hand. Her eyes lit up as she saw the gushing eruption of jism. The thick white goo shot into the whisky at the bottom of the cup.

She worked him until he had gone dry, and then she cleaned his cock with her tongue, licking away the last dripping gob of spunk as it emerged from his piss-slit.

"Now it's your turn," she said to Bob, crawling toward him on her knees. She had the cup in one hand and she was licking her lips.

He held his prick out, and she covered it with her mouth, sliding down almost to his balls in one hungry swallow. He fucked into her mouth. He was obviously on the verge of coming, too.

She could feel Jim Murray's eyes on her from the rear. She hoped he liked what he was seeing. She knew he had liked what she'd

given him in his office.

"You gonna come for me?" she asked Bob, looking up at him. "You gonna fill my cup with your milk, baby?"

He stuck the end of his cock into the top of the cup and said, "Oh, shit!"

His prick bounced around inside the paper cup, almost knocking it out of Ellen's hand. She grabbed his prick and finished milking it.

He was dry, but he was still hard, and Ellen smiled. She rocked back on her heels and looked up at the two young men. "Cheers again, guys!"

She swirled the mixture of cum and whisky in the cup until it blended, and then she poured it all down her throat in one hungry swallow.

"Now," she said, standing up, "since you guys are still hard – and I mean hard – I suppose you'd like to fuck me!"

Chapter 10

"On the other hand," Ellen said, stepping back, "a couple of big horny guys like you, maybe you might want to do all kinds of wicked things to me. Like a gang-bang, or maybe even both of you fucking me at the same time. You wouldn't have anything like that in mind, now, would you?"

"Who, us?" Bob said, bouncing one of her tits in the palm of his work-roughened hand. He pinched gently at her pink nipple, lengthening it between his fingers. Ellen sighed and shoved her tit into his grasp. "Would we do anything like that to a babe like you? You got us all wrong! We're gentlemen!"

"Right," Randy said, fingering her pussy once more. He worked into her wet hole, sliding his digit in and out. Ellen felt the delicious friction, and her cunt began to moisten a bit more, her clit pulsating with desire. "Just because you walk in off the street and suck us both off, it doesn't mean we're gonna treat you like some kind of wild slut!"

Jim Murray was still watching, a fresh cigarette between his lips. He lit it and then took a sip of whisky.

The room was not designed with orgies in mind. There was sawdust everywhere and it smelled of pine and motor oil. A single bulb with a white shade hung from overhead, casting a bright glare over the area. The floor was concrete, both rough and cold, and there was nothing remotely resembling a bed anywhere. The card table was too rickety for fucking, so it had to be the floor.

"I'll be on top," Ellen said. She tapped Randy on the chest. "You were the first to squirt.

You should be recharged by now. On your ass, stud, and let me have that prick of yours!"

He put his jeans under his ass and lay down on them. His cock wasn't entirely stiff, but it was pretty close. Ellen squatted above him, using both hands to work his cock. She felt it stiffening between her busy palms and smiled.

"That's what I want," she said. "Let's fuck!"

She moved the tip of his prick through her sopping wet pussy-hair. She hadn't realized how wet she was until she heard the squashing noise his cock made. He thrust upward as soon as he felt her succulent wetness on his prick.

His cock entered her, shoving, but she lifted upward, not quite ready to swallow him yet. She wanted a fucking, but there was an element of tease in her character she had never known was there before, and she was rather enjoying the sensation.

Ellen slid up and down, just lipping his prick with her pussy. He was breathing hard, thrusting as best he could, but she controlled the action and she only let him go as deep into her cunt as she wanted. The promise of his hard prick up her pussy made her skin crawl with anticipation, but it was nearly as much fun teasing and tantalizing herself as to do it to him.

She came down slowly, engulfing Randy's

cock without warning.

"Oh, baby!" he gasped, shoving up to meet her. The bulging meat of his cock spread the snugness of her pussy walls, and the wetness flowed down her cunt to moisten his progress.

She sank down until she could drop no farther. Now her cunt was stuffed full of his cock.

Ellen rocked atop him, relishing the feel of his cock in her pussy. His hands were all over her body. He really seemed to like her tits. She really liked the way he liked them. Leaning forward, she fed them to the kid. He sucked like a baby starved for milk, and she was sorry as hell she couldn't let him have any.

"Gimme another drink of that whisky," she said, and Bob handed her the bottle.

She slopped the booze into her mouth, some of it spilling down her chin and onto her tits. She felt warm and wild and willing.

"Now I want your cock," she said to Bob, returning the bottle.

He was quick to give it. She sucked him in, blowing wetly around his prick while she fucked Randy's cock in and out of her dripping cunt.

His cock fattened inside her mouth, and she moved back and forth on it in long thirsty swallows. Now that she'd actually done it a few times, she found that it wasn't all that tough to deep-throat a cock, even a big one like Bob's.

"How about you, dude?" she called to Jim Murray. "These guys say you're too ancient to get it up. You don't look so old to me. Bet you have one big prick in those pants. Why not come over and show it to me?"

"Nah," he said. "I really am too old. Anyway, baby, I think you're much too wild for me. Us old guys have to take it easy, you know? I think I'll just watch."

"Your loss," she said, going down on Bob's prick again. She took the bottle from his hands and poured some booze on his cock, slurping it off the skin.

She was bouncing hard on Randy's cock now, getting a sweet hot ride from it. She took him deep, her cunt grinding against his balls. She wished she could open her cunt wide enough to suck his balls up her cunt along with his long cock.

She squirmed, making her clit throb as it scraped his cock-hair, and she felt fresh oozes of wetness down the channel of her pussy. His cock kept fucking in and out of her, and she kept gulping it with the muscles of her aroused cunt while she fed on the engorged length of his friend's prick.

"Mmmmmm!" she moaned, licking her lips and rubbing Bob's cock all over her face. "I thought you guys said something about double-fucking me!"

"You serious?" Bob asked. "Oh, shit, baby, I knew I had the right instinct when I didn't call in sick tonight!"

He came around behind her as she continued to fuck his friend. He felt her up from the rear, and she sat upright, easing herself back against him. His hands were full of her tits, and he was chewing on her neck, her ears, and her shoulders. She could feel his strong hard cock bumping against her ass. Ellen had no idea if she could actually take on two guys at the same time, but she was too drunk and too excited to care.

"Fuck me in the ass while Randy rams my cunt," she said to Bob, surprising herself as usual by her coarse language, "I want that cock of yours stirring my shit!"

He cupped her ass and hefted the cheeks, seeking her asshole with his finger. She was bouncing so hard on Randy that it was difficult for him to get a grip, but suddenly he was there. His finger speared straight into her shitter!

Ellen yelped and almost jumped straight off Randy's prick. She'd been fucked in the pussy all right, and recently she'd been fucked up the ass, but never simultaneously, and even the feel of Bob's finger in her ass, thrusting along with the slam of Randy's cock up her cunt, was a shocking surprise.

She leaned forward, raising her ass,

slowing down her rhythm on Randy's cock.

"Jesus, you're tight!" Bob gasped. "I figured a whore's asshole for being as big as a barn door! Don't feel like this baby's ever been used for anything but farting!"

He slowly finger-fucked her, spreading the tautness, and she swayed and moaned in response.

Bob moved his finger more vigorously, prodding as deeply into Ellen's asshole as he could thrust, rotating the fingers as he moved them in and out. She bit her lip and squirmed atop Randy's pussy-piercing prick, and she gasped when Bob added two more fingers.

They didn't feel quite as big as Marlon's cock had done, but they were impressive as hell, and she writhed under their steady, relentless attack. She moved forward and back, keeping Randy's prick busy inside her snug cunt. Looking back over her shoulder at Bob, she said in a defiant voice, "Well, dude, are you just gonna play with it, or do you intend to fuck it too?"

"I'm gonna fuck it," Bob said. He pulled his fingers out, and before her asshole had had time to contract, he thrust his cock into the dilated opening.

She couldn't keep from screaming when his cock pierced her. Even though he'd reamed her with his fingers and gotten her shitter ready, there was no way she could have been prepared for the sudden stabbing plunge of his prick up her ass.

He was fat-cocked, and his prick was a lot bigger than his fingers.

The pressure of Randy's cock in her cunt made her ass even tighter than it was by nature, but Bob was totally intent on fucking Ellen's shit-hole, and he just rammed her with his cock until it was fully imbedded. Randy paused momentarily beneath her, just marking time with his prick, allowing Bob the full pleasure of splitting Ellen's asshole.

But it wouldn't have been human for him to be motionless beneath her forever. Bob was fucking hard, and Ellen rocked before his savage ass-busting attack. Randy grabbed Ellen's swaying tits and started to fuck her pussy, really pouring on the cock this time.

She was pinned between them, a slave to their desires. Bob hunched over her from the rear, his strong arms encircling her while he fucked her shit-hole, giving her all she had asked for and more. Randy slurped and bit her big, stiff nipples, squirming to shove his prick up her cunt again and again, matching his buddy stroke for stroke.

Maybe it was the whisky. Maybe it was the fucking. Maybe it was just the fact that she knew Jim Murray was sitting over by the table, watching everything the guys did to her! Ellen couldn't hold back her orgasm.

It hit her like an express train and she screamed, exploding between the two hard-fucking boys.

They didn't stop. They kept on pounding her with their savage cocks, filling her fuck-holes again and again.

"Ohhh, you bastards!" she moaned. "You dirty, ass-reaming, pussy-fucking bastards! Make me come! Make me come all over your hard cocks! Shoot me full of your cum! Fuck me till your spunk runs out of my goddamn ears!"

Bob's only answer was to shove his prick so far up her ass that she could almost taste it on the back of her tongue. He rabbit-fucked her asshole in a series of almost savage thrusts, each of them sending Ellen over the edge in a brand new way. Randy kept pushing his cock up her cunt, but he was simply keeping the stewpot bubbling while Bob finished her off.

"Here it comes, baby!" Bob growled. "Put your fingers in your ears!"

She felt his cock balloon inside her ass as it prepared to squirt, and she knew it would be a blasting orgasm. She rocked hard, banging his groin with her ass, the jiggle of her asscheeks slapping continuously against his belly urging him to let his cum fly.

He shoved his prick all the way into her, and it went off like a depth charge. She stiffened and revelled in the ecstatic eruption of his cock, allowing his release to merge with her own emotions and bring her orgasm to even higher levels.

Then Randy's prick gushed inside Ellen's pussy, and she collapsed, the two boys equally limp above her and beneath her, their bodies melting into a heap on the floor.

"That was something else, baby," Bob said to her as she got into her clothes. Ellen was wobbly on her feet, but she felt fantastic. Even if she was still pretty drunk. "Mmm, that fucking was worth more than a drink! Hey, I know! Come on, guys!"

The four of them went out into the sawmill, Jim Murray following.

"Coming back this way soon?" Bob asked. "Any time you do, you've got a real fan club here."

"I think I better give her a ride home," Jim Murray said. "She's too fucking drunk to drive. Hell, she can hardly stand up!"

Ellen wasn't that drunk and started to protest, but as he led her outside he squeezed her arm meaningfully and she knew what he meant. Randy and Bob came to say goodbye. Ellen got in, and Jim slid behind the wheel.

"I'll be by tomorrow some time," he said to the boys as they drove off.

* * *

When they arrived at the Cabin, they had

fixed themselves another drink from the well-stocked bar. Ellen had found some stuff in the Deepfreeze and had cooked them a late-night snack. She had suggested that they turn in and Jim readily agreed.

"Jesus," Ellen said, soaking in the tub. Murray sat on the toilet seat, smoking a last cigarette. "That was something else."

She stood up, water running down her body. Jim handed her a towel and she wiped it lazily over her body as she stood on the rug by the tub. She knotted the towel around her body and looked at him archly.

"I want to ask you a question: why didn't you join the guys? We could have had a four-way. Maybe I could have blown you while they fucked me. I've never tried it with three guys at once."

"I don't often go for orgies," he said. "Besides, I wanted to watch you getting fucked. It was kinda horny."

He grinned.

"What about you?" he asked, putting out his cigarette. "I gather you've been out getting a little revenge on your husband."

Ellen smiled. That was certainly one way to describe it. She moved past Murray. He caught her by the wrist and turned her around.

"What do you plan to do about him?"

"I'm not sure just yet. He's still in Los Angeles with that slut," she said.

The back of his hand brushed the underside of her lovely tits, moving up and over the nipples. Ellen smiled. It felt pretty good.

"I met a couple tonight," she said. "They had a strange way of spicing up their marriage. It got me thinking about Meredith and me. I guess I might still love him. I wouldn't be so pissed off at him if I didn't care. When he gets back from Los Angeles, I think I'm going to confront him with what I know, and then we'll just have to reach an understanding. Do you know I even ate pussy tonight? I never did that before. I liked it. I think I could even enjoy eating the pussy of that redheaded slut my husband's been fucking around with. It might just save our marriage."

"Do you want to save your marriage? Do you think it's really worth saving?"

She didn't answer him directly but undid the towel and let it slide down her body. Her quivering tits seemed to leap out at him. She looked up hungrily towards him and although Jim Murray's slate-grey eyes never seemed to give much away, she thought she detected a sadness there that hadn't existed before.

"You know," she said, "maybe it would help me – with Meredith, I mean – if I… if we… fucked once more. I mean, getting fucked by some total stranger, well, total strangers, and loving the shit out of it is one thing. But I know you now, Jim Murray, and

I like you, too. If it weren't for all this mess, well, we might have had something going..." She let the words die away, and looking closely at his rugged features, thought she could read just a hint of pain there, a touch of bitterness, even.

Jim gave her a cryptic smile.

"So what are we waiting for, you cock-happy bitch?" He dealt her a playful slap on the ass. "Why don't you take a douche and an enema and gargle a little? I'll be waiting for you in the bedroom. And after what I saw back at the sawmill, why hell, I could fuck you all night."

* * *

When Ellen came into the bedroom, all shined and powdered and fresh as spring, Jim was lying on the bed in his boxer shorts. The tip of his cock was showing through the slit at the front. Ellen remembered how good it had tasted, and how good it had felt fucking her. She smiled and eased onto the bed alongside him.

He moved down her body with hands and mouth, arousing every part of her. As he fed on her tits, her belly, as his mouth worked down to the pouting slice of her pussy, she began to feel more certain that, at the very least, Murray seemed to have a bit of a crush on her. There was a distinctly romantic twist to the way his tongue flicked her stiffened clit and dipped into the puckered mouth of her cunt.

He got his finger into her pussy, fucking it slowly in and out while he nibbled on her cunt. It was a sensuous and sensitive approach, and she could not resist. Twisting around, she took his cock in her hands, then started to lick around the foreskin.

Her mouth ovalled, the lips red and moist and willing. She sucked him inside, loving him friskily with her tongue as she moved the big, shining head of his cock in and out of the retracting foreskin. His tongue was deep in her pussy now, his cunt-wet finger stroking softly over the hardened button of her clit as he pulled back on her springy bush hair to expose the sassy little bean of pink flesh. Each caress sent fresh shivers of delight racing through Ellen.

Her hands worked on the shaft of his cock while her mouth nursed at his knob. She wanted to feel his jizz squirting across her tongue, but she also craved to feel that hard firm cock thrusting hotly and wildly inside her pussy.

"Oh, let's fuck," she said, raising her lips from his cock. "I really think I need to be fucked again."

"That makes two of us," Jim Murray said. He turned, sliding up against Ellen, his eager hands all over her body.

She opened herself to his caresses, covering his hands as they fondled her tits. She made him pinch the stiff nipples, and he lifted them to her face so she could lick and suck at them too. Their tongues duelled over the points of her tits.

She guided his fingers down to her wet cunt, easing them into her fuck-hole so she could milk them with her cunt muscles and prove just how ready and excited she really was.

He turned Ellen over onto her side and pushed against her from the rear. She threw a leg back over him, then reached down between her legs to trap his prick in her hand. She stroked it, adoring the firm strength of his cock, and then she pulled it to her waiting pussy. Ellen groaned as his huge, stiff prick sank home.

"Oh, fuck me now!" she whispered, her body pulsating to the rhythm of his driving cock.

He fucked into her, picking up speed.

Murray held her tits. She leaned her face back to kiss him, moaning into his mouth, as the frenzy of his stabbing cock grew more and more irresistible. She frigged her pussy while she received his prick, and her clit swelled under her briskly rubbing fingers. Fuck-juice oozed from her cunt, soaking his prick as it moved in and out.

"Just for old time's sake?" she said, sliding forward, her cunt pulling way from Murray's cock. She lifted her leg and spread her asscheeks, baring her shit-hole. He smiled, guiding his prick in the direction she wanted.

She was getting used to ass-fucking now, it seemed. He fumbled a moment, but her ass-ring quickly sucked him in, and she gave a howling cry of joy as her shit-tube was filled with his throbbing cock.

He was the first guy who'd ever fucked her ass, taken her backdoor virginity. She'd always have a soft spot for him. His cock pumped energetically into that soft spot, and Ellen kept on squeezing and flicking her clit, soaking her fingers in the juices that leaked and dribbled from her pussy.

Her world had fallen apart only this week, but with her asshole full of Jim Murray's cock and her cunt boiling beneath her fingers, she felt safe and secure and confident once again. It didn't matter what happened when Meredith came back from Los Angeles and she confronted him with the truth.

Ellen had looked inside herself, and she was pleased with what she had found there. Another orgasm was simmering in her cunt, and it looked like tomorrow would be a very nice day.

Eventually they fell asleep, curled up together on the big bed.

Chapter 11

Ellen was alone in the Cabin cooking ham and eggs for breakfast when she saw Meredith and Nancy drive up. Jim had gone to the local store to buy cigarettes.

She decided to take control of the situation and strode out to the car, full of anger and determination.

"You and I need to talk, Meredith."

Nancy opened her mouth to say something, but Ellen didn't give her a chance.

"You, stay in the car, bitch. Just keep your big freckly tits out of this," she snapped at Nancy.

Husband and wife walked beyond the Cabin down to the more neutral ground of the bridge across the river. Meredith's normally handsome features appeared strained and grim as she gave him a full catalogue of his infidelities.

"I'm sorry, Ellen, I should have told you earlier."

"Told me what, exactly, Meredith?"

"That I'm not in love with you any more. I'm in love with Nancy."

"Oh, so you're going to throw away

everything we had for a quick crack at the town slut. I hear she's screwed half the men in Wenatchee. You're happening on the scene a little late in the day aren't you? And what about your career? Do you want to throw all that away too?"

Meredith's face took on a hateful, almost demonic, mien.

"Oh no, Ellen. I don't intend to throw anything away. Well, nothing that's worth keeping."

Ellen realised that she had touched a raw nerve and suddenly she began to feel an aura of evil menace emanating from her husband. To her alarm she realised that they had reached halfway across the old wooden bridge. She turned and started to walk back to the Cabin. But Meredith was quicker than her and, grabbing her by the arm, slammed her hard against the bridge's flimsy handrail. The wood, certainly old and possibly even rotten, instantly gave way and, with a little shriek of horror, Ellen found herself falling into space. To this day, she cannot remember how she did it, but as she fell, she grabbed at anything within her reach and managed to hold on to the long metal strip at the base of the handrail.

Forty feet below she could see the brown, swirling waters of the river as it churned towards the boulder-strewn rapids. She knew that even if she survived the fall, before she could even scream for help she would be dashed to pieces against the rocks. She had to hold on, even though the thin strip of metal was cutting into her fingers now and starting to hurt like hell.

Her husband looked down at her. He didn't seem inclined to help, indeed, one of his boots rested lightly on top of her cramped fingers.

"I'm sorry, honey. It's too late. If you go over now it's going to look like a tragic accident. And unless you've changed your will, after your funeral I'm going to be a very rich man indeed. Then, with an appropriate period of mourning of course, Nancy and I will fall in love and get married. Oh sure, people will have their doubts. But they'll never be able to prove a fucking thing." He laughed and increased the pressure of his boot on her fingers at the same time as bringing his other foot to rest on her other hand. She was slowly losing the feeling in both hands.

"You're an utter fool, Meredith. Too many people know about you and Nancy. They'll put two and two together and you'll end up in the electric chair."

Meredith was about to come back with a snappy answer when he noticed that his soon-to-be-deceased wife was grinning back at him. He found that puzzling. Definitely not the face of one about to meet her Maker, he thought. He looked behind him and for a split second he saw the burly figure of Jim Murray, one step behind him and swinging a heavy axe haft down towards his cranium.

* * *

Much later, Meredith woke up with a splitting headache. He tried to feel where his head hurt most, but discovered that his hands were tied. He also found that, as well as being trussed like a Thanksgiving turkey, he was stark naked. But he wasn't tied in a conventional way, whoever had done this had simply tied each of his wrists to each of his ankles. He tested the knots, but they had been expertly done with something resembling a nylon washing line.

"This is a helluva mess you've got us into, Meredith."

He looked up and saw that he was in the Cabin's big living room. Nancy was equally naked and tied in an identical way, only she sat on the deep pile carpet with her back to one of the plush sofas. She looked very pissed.

"Hey, Nance. I didn't know it was going to turn out like this. What can I say – I'm sorry."

"You tried to kill your wife just now – and nearly succeeded," she spat at him bitterly. "What were you even thinking of? Now they'll probably kill us."

She started to sob uncontrollably.

"I don't think they will, Nancy," he replied, without much conviction.

At that moment a small group entered the Cabin's big living room. There was Ellen and Jim Murray. The two sawmill boys: Randy and Bob. And bringing up the rear, was Ellen's Oriental friend, Suzie. Suzie was carrying a riding crop and an enormous black phallus that dangled from some sort of harness contraption. They all started to undress. It was payback time.

"Get that bitch on her knees. No, wait. I'll do it."

And Ellen, now magnificently naked, strode over to where Nancy was slumped against the sofa, her coppery pubic bush carelessly displayed between her open legs. Taking a great handful of her thick red hair at the back of her head, she yanked the bound and blubbering girl forwards so that she fell on her face and outsize tits, her ass sticking up. Meanwhile, Randy was manhandling Meredith into the same position so that effectively the illicit lovers knelt side by side, with their asses in the air, like supplicants at some weird religious ceremony. The terrified pair looked vulnerable and more than a little absurd.

Although Ellen had no clear idea just how she was going to punish her husband and his slut of a girlfriend, it occurred to her that she should defer to Suzie's greater expertise in this area. When she had called her forty-five minutes ago, Suzie had sounded almost indecently excited at the prospect of helping her out.

"Honey, I have just the equipment for this. I love punishing a man... and a girl too, come to think of it! Be with you as soon as I can."

Jim had then made a call to his buddies at the sawmill and they had been astonished when they heard the name of the beautiful broad they had pleasured last night; nevertheless, they were keen as mustard to come over and help out.

Now they were all naked as sin apart from Suzie who wore a black leather peekaboo bra and a bottom made of the same material. She tested the riding crop in her hand with a little 'swish' and a loud 'thwack'.

"Ladies first. How many strokes do you want me to give the slut?" she asked Ellen, grinning.

"Depends how hard you hit, but oh, I should say a dozen, six on each cheek. Then I want the boys to fuck her in the ass. Of course, she loves that, so hard as you can, boys. I'd hate for Nancy to be disappointed."

By this time, Nancy was almost hysterical with fear. She was gibbering, promising anything to anybody and struggling to get up from her awkward position. The sawmill boys held her down and Suzie wasted no time at all in giving her twelve measured strokes of the crop. Nancy screamed at first, but then took each hit with a sort of miserable whimper. The Oriental was a most consummate mistress of her craft; the strokes were applied with incredible accuracy and timing, and the red weals crisscrossed almost geometrically on poor Nancy's jerking, bouncing buttocks. The last two stripes were hardest and Ellen could see tiny beads of red forming. Suzie saw this too and quickly got down on her hands and knees to lick the blood of her sobbing victim.

"How many for this jerk?" asked Suzie pointing at Meredith with her crop.

"Oh, two dozen for him. And hard ones, too. Think you're man enough to take your medicine, Meredith? If not, we can always hold you down."

"Just get the fuck on with it, you crazy bitches," was all that Meredith could say in reply, spitting the words out with as much defiance as he could muster.

In the end, Bob and Jim had to hold him down as Meredith screamed and struggled like a wild thing. Randy was already lustily fucking a whimpering Nancy in the ass and delightedly mistreating her enormous, dangling breasts.

Suzie was merciless and by the time she

had finished, the buttocks of Ellen's husband were crisscrossed with angry red weals, some of which were bleeding. The man himself was blubbering pathetically.

"Just feel the bitch's cunt!" gasped Randy in wonder, as he neared his climax and got ready to shoot his load into Nancy's rectum.

"She's wet as a swamp on a rainy day!"

On hearing this, Ellen couldn't resist feeling the redhead's copper-haired slit. It oozed cunt cream and, judging by the look of bliss on Nancy's face and the way she thrust her striped asscheeks back at Randy, she was beginning to really love the treatment she was getting. An idea came to Ellen, but she wanted everyone to fuck Nancy in the ass before the grand finale. Bob was next, then finally Jim.

Suzie, who had now stripped completely and strapped on the huge black rubber dildo, was positioning herself between Meredith's legs. She was humane enough to spit over the dark, hairy pucker between his bleeding buns and apply more saliva to the tip of her menacing black weapon, but this was hardly adequate lubrication for the monster that she started to gradually thrust deeper and deeper into his utterly unprotected, vulnerable anus.

Meredith whimpered and moaned in pain and, by looking his left, he became aware of Jim getting ready to anally fuck the love of his life with the biggest cock he'd ever seen in his life.

Nancy screamed and writhed when she felt the size of Jim's big cock in her ass, and begged him to finish soon, but he was implacable and took his time, finally unloading a massive quantity of sperm up her delectable backside adding to the two deposits already made by his pals.

Meredith Fielding was a broken man and Ellen almost felt sorry for her would-be murderer. But she stiffened her resolve and asked Suzie to pull out of his forever-stretched asshole.

Ellen now gave instructions in a terse, authoritative voice.

"Untie them both. Lie Meredith on his back. Now you, cunt," and here she indicated Nancy, "straddle his face so that he can eat out your nasty little ass. Why Meredith, dear, you must like that idea, because you have quite an impressive hard-on there. That's just as well, because I'm going to fuck you, darling, for the very last time…"

With Nancy already in position and facing her above her prone husband, Ellen climbed on top of her husband and inserted his cock into her dripping cunt. "Mmm… that's good, oh yes that's sooo good!" she purred. "You know Meredith, you never fucked me in the ass, did you. Well, you never will, either.

Too bad, because now we've both lost our backdoor cherries. But I want you to feel me getting it in the shitter. It's so good when he does it, too. He's got a nicer cock than yours, and it's bigger, too. Come on Jim, darling man, stir my shit for me... give it to me up my turd-tube... fuck my fucking asshole!"

The beautiful heiress was getting off on using the most vulgar words and phrases that she knew and they acted as an aphrodisiac for Jim, whose cock was stiffer than he'd ever known it. Gently he eased it up past Ellen's anal ring and deep into the buttery depths of her rectal cavity. She gave the base of his cock a special welcoming squeeze with her asshole. He could feel her husband's hard dick through the thin membrane that separated ass and cunt. He started to fuck in strong, rhythmic strokes, his heavy balls slapping down against Meredith's tight scrotal sack.

Ellen felt more powerful, more sexually fulfilled than ever before in her entire existence. She was fucking one man out of her life forever at the same time as fucking another into it, she was pretty sure.

Above Meredith's sucking mouth, Nancy started to climax and lost control: a torrent of tainted sperm gushed from her gaping, incontinent hole to cover her lover's face and mouth. It was the final humiliation. Above him Nancy bucked and swayed in ecstasy;

Ellen, too, was about to experience a massive orgasm, thrusting herself down upon the two hard rods of flesh that penetrated her again and again. As it hit her, she flailed her arms around and, by mistake, slapped Nancy's enormous tits. It felt so good that as she shook and shuddered with prolonged orgasmic blasts in her cunt and ass, she started to rain slaps down on the redhead's vulnerable breasts. When she tired of this she started to pinch the girl's stiff, rubbery nipples so hard and painfully that they almost glowed red. Whether Nancy liked Ellen's sadistic treatment of her enormous hooters or not was hard to say, but she continued to slide her sperm-saturated, gooey crotch over Meredith's upturned face, almost suffocating him in the process. Despite his struggles she allowed him no chance of escaping from the vice-like grip of her thighs.

Meanwhile Suzie had discovered the sawmill boys' talent for a simultaneous ass and pussy fuck and the delicate Oriental gasped with pleasure as they ploughed both her tight holes, buffeting her slender form as they sandwiched it between their young, muscular bodies.

Just as Ellen's climax started to subside, she felt her husband tense beneath her. His cock grew even stiffer for a few seconds and a series of small groans emanated from his

mouth; she knew that he was shooting his last ever spurts of cum inside her. And a few seconds later, behind her, Jim groaned and held her very still by the hips as he shook and shuddered. She milked him with her sphincter as he came, trying to maximise his obvious pleasure. A soft nuzzling of her neck rewarded her, something he knew she adored.

The big man disengaged, his softening penis exiting her bowels with a sucking, liquid sound. Little gushes of sperm splattered Meredith's stomach and pubic hair as she stood up. He looked a complete mess.

The room fell silent and Ellen finally spoke in a low, but authoritative voice.

She told Meredith and Nancy that they could leave and that the police would not be told about his attempt to kill her, but that if they ever came within two hundred miles of the Cabin, their own lives would be in danger. Meredith was not to contest the divorce suit that Ellen would bring against him in the next few days, nor was he to expect a single cent of her fortune. His resignation from his job and from the board of Roeberds was to be in writing and delivered to the head office in Wenatchee tomorrow. Otherwise… and she indicated the three smiling, burly men beside her.

As the miscreants' car sped down the drive, an exhausted but radiant Ellen hugged Jim. They kissed passionately and she felt his rigid sex stir against the soft flesh of her belly.

The others got dressed, made their farewells, and they all promised to get back together soon.

When at last they were alone, Ellen cuddled up to Jim on the big sofa.

"So, would you like to get together for another orgy with the boys and Suzie sometime soon?" she asked, archly.

"Naahh. It's not really my style. But then if it was just Suzie and you and me, well, we could have some fun there, I guess!" And Jim laughed long and loud and Ellen punched him playfully, but hard.

The End

Just a few of our many titles for sale...

Los Angeles Girl & Punishment for Claudia
Special double edition. Model and virgin, Della, finds herself giving more than she wants to on her photo-shoots in *Los Angeles Girl*. Claudia is a Nazi spy in wartime USA with a penchant for spanking, being spanked and submissive sex in *Punishment for Claudia*.

£12.50

In Deep
Richard and Bridget O'Connell are happily married. But Richard is hiding a dark secret and when his best friend, Dan Masters, discovers this, he and his wife use their knowledge to blackmail Bridget. Gradually, they suck the couple into a web of forbidden lust. How can they escape? And do they want to?

£7.50

Bondi Beach Orgy
Beautiful and innocent Susan Kempford is determined to save her virginity for her wedding night. Lance Tomlinson has other ideas. But taking Susan's virginity is not enough for Lance, and with some help from his friends and gorgeous cousin, he subjects Susan to increasingly debauched ordeals.

£7.50

Ranchers' Dirty Wives
When Danny McCluskie brings his gorgeous, virginal, young bride Billy Jo to his family's cattle ranch in Texas, the scene is set for marital bliss. Until Danny has a riding fall and is laid up for a month. Enter three horny brother-in-laws, a megalomaniac ranch manager and others determined to seduce her.

£9.50

Turkish Delight
After being cruelly raped by her callous husband on her honeymoon, Lucy Dean finds herself adrift in one of the most exciting and dangerous cities in the world: Istanbul. Drugged and abducted, she faces a life of sexual slavery, but first she must be taught the tricks of the trade.

£7.50

Orderline: 0800 026 25 24
Customer Service: 020 7736 5800
Email: eros@eroticprints.org

EPS

WWW.EROTICPRINTS.ORG